Way In Over
Our heads

Way In Over Our Heads

A Novel By

EURAL J. BLACK

PUBLISHER'S NOTE:

This book is inspired by true events.

All rights reserved, including the right of reproduction in whole or part in any form.

All Copyrights Reserved © 2022 by Eural J. Black

TABLE OF CONTENTS

Acknowledgement 1

Chapter 1 3

Chapter 2 6

Chapter 3 10

Chapter 4 18

Chapter 5 23

Chapter 6 27

Chapter 7 30

Chapter 8 35

Chapter 9 47

Chapter 10 51

Chapter 11 54

Chapter 12 59

Chapter 13 67

Chapter 14 70

Chapter 15..81

Chapter 16..84

Chapter 17..86

Chapter 18..89

Chapter 19..97

Chapter 20..99

Chapter 21..103

Chapter 22..105

Chapter 23..109

Chapter 25..112

Acknowledgement

I must give GOD all praise, glory, and honor. HE says all good things come from HIM, and that HE disciplines those HE loves. I thank HIM for the good things, and ask HIM for strength to deal with the discipline. Thank GOD for HIS place in my life and HIS plans for my life.

I must thank GOD for my wife, the "helper" HE placed in my life. Sher had the fortitude to keep our family together in the toughest of times and she never loss her equilibrium.

Madison, Eural, and Justyce, your dad failed you. I implore you to put your faith in the ONE who will never fail you.

I want to thank the men who subsisted with me at Beckley Federal Correctional Institution especially the guys in Poplar A Upper. Thank you for your patience while I used the computer to type my story. The world needs to hear your story too.

There are so many more people in my life who I owe thanks to. Some have gone on to glory, and others continue to motivate and inspire me. Thank you very much.

Chapter 1

I was sitting in roll call thinking about Savanna when my friend June came and plopped down next to me.

"I wonder what the watch commander is going to wear today" he said.

Savanna and I were separated, it was mostly my fault and I was eager to run and call her. I was thinking of new ways to inject emotions unto my same old tired apologies. She said they were empty apologies, that she had heard them before from me, and that she was tired of hearing them. But I still had to try.

June and I were new young police officers who started our careers on the Southeast side of Chicago. We bounced around working with other officers but wanted to be partners. Our lieutenant said he'd partner us up when the opportunity presented itself. On this day we weren't working together. I was working with a white police woman and we were working in an area of the district that black police officers were neither regularly assigned to nor did we live in.

Our watch commander that day wore a cowboy hat, a Hawaiian shirt, cowboy boots and a toy gun in a holster to roll call. When he called my name, I answered "here." When he called my partner's name, she said, "Present sir." He looked over his glasses at us and marked something down on his paper. After roll call I ran to the telephone to call Savanna. While I was on the telephone, I noticed Ollie "Rap" Reynolds trying to get my attention. He was this huge, imposing black police officer who always talked about black awareness and black consciousness, black that and black that. When my call was over he approached me and said I'd been reassigned to work with him. I said okay, grabbed my things and followed him to our car. When we got to the car he said, "Did you see what the watch commander had on? He only started wearing stuff like that since the new black Commander was appointed. When he was called out on it, him and a rabble of other white police officers became part of a resistance, acting in defiance, and not recognizing or acknowledging him as their boss. They refuse to accept the tides of change. Harold Washington ain't been dead for 5 years yet but they want to turn back the hands of time. And the reason you were reassigned is because they don't want us working with white police women. It happened to me too. They'll assign a sista with a white boy in a minute but they won't put us with them white girls. Eight hours in a car is a lot of time to get to know a person."

We got a call to assist a citizen in an area of the district where mostly white folks lived. When we got there an elderly white woman saw us coming, stuck her head out of her door and said, "I didn't call you!" and slammed her door. Reynolds looked at me and shrugged his shoulders. We told the dispatcher that the woman refused service and we left. A few minutes later the dispatcher said the woman called again and asked us to go back to the house. Another officer said he'd go too because he was familiar with the woman. When we went back, she reiterated that she did not call us. When she saw the other police officer, a white officer, she came out on the porch and talked to him. After their talk he said, "They usually don't assign black police officers to this sector so it must've surprised her to see you guys here. She's just a lonely old widow who wanted to talk to a police officer, just not y'all. She doesn't trust black police officers."

June was Puerto Rican and he hated it when I called him Mexican. I had a bad habit of doing that. I couldn't tell the difference. They all looked the same to me. He said that Mexicans felt like they were better than other Latinos even though most of them were illegals. June called everybody niggas. He called Latino's niggas. He called Black people niggas, and he called white folks' niggas. "You're an educated man" I said "You can't go around calling everybody niggas." He said it was cool because him and his people were niggas too.

June was my best friend in the department and as partners we shared a lot of our personal lives. I told him about my separation from Savanna, how I screwed things up, that she was seeing somebody else, and that I wanted to get back together again. He told me about a new young lady he met and he wanted me to meet her. June often offered raw unsolicited marital advice that was never constructive.

"I know you want to get back with Savanna but just in case she dumps you because likes having sex with the new guy, you might want to think about moving on."

CHAPTER 2

Sometimes after work we'd sit in the police parking lot and have a few drinks. Other times we'd go and drink with the white officers at a bar of their choosing. The new girl June met, Dorena, was a bartender at a club in Humboldt Park or Logan Square and he wanted me to socialize with them in their milieu. The night I was suppose to meet him I go lost. I wasn't familiar with the Northwest side of the city. I called him and he directed me to the bar. When I got there, he looked at me funny. I said, "What's wrong?" June said, "That's a peculiar looking shirt you got on." We went into the bar and I asked him where the young lady was. He said she hadn't got there yet so we sat down at the bar and ordered some drinks. A few minutes later she came in and waved at us. She brought two friends with her, one who looked like she could have been her twin and the other one looked like she just ate a set of twins. He introduced me to Dorena and she introduced us to her friends. All Puerto Ricans. June and I got our drinks and we all went to a table. Dorena went behind the bar and talked to her co-workers for a minute then came back and said that the appetizers for the night were on her. The big girl was loud, crass, and obnoxious. She talked about everybody, what they wore and how they looked. Like June they called everybody niggas.

And their Ebonics was better than mines. She chain-smoked Newport 100 cigarettes and was a rude ungulated drunk who had us laughing all night. After about 30 minutes June and Dorena went to another table and talked privately. I think they were trying to set me up with that heafer. The two women talked amongst themselves in English but switched mid-sentence to Spanish. They kept referring to me as El Negro and Prieto. I didn't know what Prieto meant but I knew what negro was. I knew they were talking about me because I was the only negro there. I think they were talking about my shirt. And somebody's breath was stinking.

The next time that June and I worked together he told me that it was not his intention to try and set me up with the big girl.

"I didn't know that Dorena was bringing people with her. She said that Jenn, the big girl, thought you was cute but weird. They probably thought you were gay because you didn't talk much and because of that funny looking shirt you had on. What was up with that?" I said, "I didn't talk because I don't like her, and about that shirt, Savanna buys my clothes but one day I was out, saw it and thought it looked cool."

June said, "Well it didn't look cool. It looked gay. And that Jenn, she was a big one wasn't she? In case you change your mind, she only has three kids and none of their fathers wants anything to do with her or them so they'd out of the way. And I don't know if noticed but somebody's breath was stinking." I said I didn't notice. Then his mood changed and he became introspective.

I said, What's up with you?"

He said, "Let me ask you a question. Dorena and I had that talk. How many sex partners would you expect a reputable young woman to have had?" I told him that I didn't know anything about Hispanic culture and he asked me about Black women. I said, "One."

He said, "No, I'm serious."

I said I was serious.

He said, "I really like this woman and I want to be with her."

"Then it shouldn't matter how many boyfriends she's had." I said.

He shot back, "Nigga you sound like a fool." It shouldn't matter–it does matter! And anyway I'm not concerned with how many boyfriends she had or with how many guys she slept with. You can have sex without sleeping. Sleep ain't got nothing to do with it. And worst of all, what if she had sex with niggas and white boys. White boys would be unacceptable."

I asked him how many different women he had sex with and he said about seven. Then I asked him if he told Dorena. He said he did and that she didn't seem fazed. Then he asked her how many dudes she has slept with. She said, "About that same number." He said he didn't like that response and it ruined his night. Since he didn't pull any punches when he offered me advice, I thought I'd give him a dose of his own medicine.

"It don't matter what culture a person comes from, If you ain't comfortable with "about that same number" then you need to run away from this woman as fast as you can." He didn't want to hear that either. He liked her a lot but, like me, thought that seven different guys was a lot. I guess it was cool for him but not for her. But who was I to judge anybody. I was a drunk and an adulterer. But he asked me for advice and I'm pretty sure he knew how I'd answer his question.

Chapter 3

Officer Hall was assigned to a foot beat in the business district on 63rd and Cottage Grove. His sergeant told him that a minivan taken in a carjacking was seen recently in the area and to be on the lookout for it.

A couple of hours later he was talking to some men outside a restaurant when he saw a minivan parked on the side street with the engine running and a woman sitting in the driver's seat. He also noticed that she was quite interested in what he was doing. He walked behind the minivan in an attempt to run the license plates but there weren't any plates on it. As he approached the minivan a man came running from a store and began shooting at him. He was able to take cover behind a truck and return fire. The man jumped in the minivan and they sped away. Backup arrived immediately but the minivan got away. It was recovered a few days later about 10 miles south in an area called the Shalom Homes.

The minivan was secured so that the crime lab could try and lift fingerprints from it. When a lieutenant from the district where the minivan was recovered found out it was there, she rode out there to talk to the people. Lieutenant Shovonne Cush grew up in the Homes, moved away when she was young, and returned to work there after she graduated from college. She wanted to serve the very community that she knew needed good dedicated police officers. She was well-known and well-respected in the community. When word got out that she was there people came from everywhere to talk to her and she addressed everything that was in her purview. She was approachable, personable, and empathetic. The community called her Lt. Smiley because of her infectious smile. She also had a reputation for being tough. One day when she was at a shopping mall, she saw a man carjacking a woman and she shot and killed him. So when she heard that the suspects of another carjacking might be hiding in the Homes she went out there to see what she could do to get them.

The police officers had their snitches working the area trying to get information on the suspects but nobody was talking. After a few days, out of respect, she requested a meeting with the shot callers--the gang leaders and the drug dealers. She wanted to appeal to their sense of decency and moral obligation to the community. She could effectively communicate with the guys on the streets as well as with the mayor, city officials, and police brass.

"I know somebody knows something" she said. "We just want to get these violent people out of our community. We all deserve to live in peace as the name of this place suggest. If you don't want to tell me where they are in a public way, get the information to me anonymously. I know you probably don't care that they shot at a police officer but they also carjacked a young mother and beat her with a gun in front of her young children. We want our seniors and children to be safe in our community. People like that are a menace and should be locked up. I implore you to help me. I'll be back tomorrow, and the day after that, and the day after that one until we get these people. Thank you for helping us."

She knew that they probably weren't going to give the suspects up but she still had to try.

No new information was coming in. Anybody who knew anything was reticent and claimed to not know anything. This was a new generation of youngsters who knew nothing about the lieutenant's reputation but they were about to find out. That was a Thursday and she told them she'd be back on the following Sunday. By that time somebody should be willing to talk.

Sunday afternoon the lieutenant and her driver went back out to the Homes. "Today in church my Pastor preached a sermon that went straight to my spirit." she said. "In Matthew's 25 it says that GOD blessed each of us with gifts and talents, first to praise, honor, and serve HIM, and also to serve others. It is a privilege to do this work and we shouldn't take it for granted. We have the power to change lives and that is exactly what we are going to do. These are our people and we are the ones who should help them. If we aren't faithful doing this work maybe somebody else will do it. Somebody who doesn't care."

"When I was a kid there was an older black police woman with salt and pepper-colored dreads who worked out here. She talked to everyone who needed to talk to her. She always had a cup of coffee in one hand and a cigarette dangling from her mouth. If she thought someone was dealing drugs from a house she'd park in front of that house. She didn't give the drug dealers or gang bangers no slack and they had the utmost respect for her. She was one tough sister and the example I'd like to follow."

When they got out to the Homes she asked the guys again if someone wanted to help her get the suspects. She was growing increasingly frustrated and agitated at their reluctance to help. She said,

"I know how this works. I know what it is. Nobody wants to be labeled a snitch. Right? That's cool. You guys ain't just letting anybody come out here and set up shop. Y'all know what's going on. We tried civility and niceties, now we're gonna do it my way. It's my understanding that you guys got the best weed on the Southside. I hear that people come from miles around to get that stuff. Check this out. We're gonna shut this thing down. Y'all have been operating with impunity for years. You guys are way too comfortable around here. See if you can get a nickel bag of weed sold around here. We're gonna completely shut this thing down. If you don't think I can do it, and if you don't think I'm serious, try me. don't f*#k with me!"

Some of the guys laughed at her, others snickered and smirked. After that she and her driver left the Homes. When they got to the car, the driver said, "Ma'am, didn't you go to church today? What's up with that profanity?"

She said, "Yeah, I know. I asked for forgiveness."

He said, "You did? I didn't hear you."'

She said, "I wasn't talking to you."

They went back to the station so she could talk to her bosses and it just so happened that the Commander was there. He was finishing up on some last-minute paperwork before his vacation started and he was just the person she needed to talk to.

"Boss, I know you're going on vacation but I need just five minutes of your time." He said, "I give you three." She told him about her plan to flood the Homes with police officers because someone was harboring the suspects to a carjacking. She said she knew the suspects were still there because the snitches told her they were but nobody was saying exactly where they were hiding. And she said she needed the additional manpower by that week. The lieutenant broke down her plan to him and he was quite impressed. He told her he'd make a few calls and would leave her a message when he got a response. He turned to leave but said, "Did you say you needed those officers this week? What's the big rush? Why the sense of urgency?" She said that the upcoming week was the first of the month and that some people bought drugs before they paid their bills and she wanted to shut down the sale of marijuana in the Homes.

That following Thursday the Lieutenant called her troops together to an outside roll call in the Homes. Outside roll calls were conducted to convey a show of force. She wanted to send a message to the community and those harboring the suspects that she meant business. The Commander could only get her 24 additional officers per watch which wound up being more than enough. That meant 12 additional cars patrolling the area per watch. The LORD will provide. The sergeant passed out mug shots of the suspects whose fingerprints were taken from the minivan. She said,

"Someone is hiding some violent suspects of a carjacking out here. Since we couldn't get any cooperation from those people who know where these people are, we're gonna shut this thing down. If they wanna sell drugs let them try and do it outside their comfort zone. Every suspicious car, truck, van, taxicab, bus; anybody who looks like they "fit the description" of a drug buyer, we're going to follow them. We don't want to harass the citizens of this community and we'll only make arrests if necessary. Everything the comes into the area, delivery trucks, U.S.P.S. mail trucks, FedEx trucks, cable trucks, ice cream trucks, and even church vans, will get an escort courtesy of the Chicago Police department. And pay particular attention to pedestrian traffic too. We want to be highly visible and we'll be here as long as it takes. I ain't got nothing better to do. What about y'all? Contrary to what they think or believe, we're the baddest gang in this city" she said drolly. I can imagine the guys looked at this thirty something year old woman and thought, they've been threatening to shut down drug sells in the Homes for years. Ain't no way she can do it. But this time it was personal. They didn't have this lieutenant to contend with.

Every police district on the Southside sent police officers to work this operation. Since June and I requested to work together the sergeant conscripted us to work this operation which had been going on for about a week when we were assigned. We worked the afternoon shift, from 3:00pm-11:00pm. That was ideal. It gave us a chance to still have a few drinks after work.

We were still fairly new police officers and we couldn't quite identify what suspicious people looked like. We mostly drove around following cars and trucks. When we saw white people we followed them, knowing that they were there to buy drugs. When they noticed us following them they drove around in circles and eventually got frustrated and left. I'm sure the citizens who lived in the Homes appreciated all the attention they got and wondered why it couldn't be like this all the time.

We saw a white guy driving a Ford Explorer looking suspicious and we followed him for a while. He was about to see how it felt to be racially profiled. We noticed him looking at us in his mirror. He was also going around in circles. He wasn't paying attention and sailed through a traffic light. That was the probable cause we needed. I put on the mars lights and pulled him over. We cautiously approached the truck and said, "Put your hands on the steering wheel where I can see them and don't move." He understood those commands and did it. I asked him for his driver's license and he shrugged his shoulders and mumbled something unintelligible. There was something about this guy that wasn't right. He seemed nervous. I asked him again, this time louder, "Where's your driver's license?" as if that was the barrier. This time he sounded Hispanic so I pressed the window button on his side and let the passenger's side window down so June could hear our conversation. June said something to him in Spanish but he still didn't respond so I got him out of the truck, patted him down and took him to our car. June searched the truck and a few minutes later he came back to the car, handcuffed the guy, and told me we were taking him into the station. June drove his truck and I followed him. June pulled into a parking space at the police station and I parked our car right behind him blocking the car it. Once before when we were going to tow a car, someone came into the police station parking lot with an extra set of keys and took the car. June got out of the truck and had a plastic Aldi's grocery bag in his hand. The guy looked dejected as we walked him into the station.

I took the guy to the interview room where arrestees were processed. There was another police officer there processing his arrestee. I sat the guy down, June put the bag on the table next to me and went to talk to our sergeant. He came back with the sergeant and showed him the contents of the bag. The sergeant looked inside the bag and said, "Wow!" Then him and June left the room. Me and the other police officer looked at each other, looked at the bag, and then looked at guy. June came back and asked me how much I thought was inside. I said how much what? He pushed the bag to me, and me and the other officer looked inside. There had to be thousands of dollars inside. June saw some marijuana in an ashtray before he saw the money and that's the reason why he was being arrested.

After all the paperwork was completed and the guy was in lock-up, the sergeant congratulated us and told us to take the rest of the day off. It was only an hour but we appreciated it. He said, "The community In the Shalom's gave up the suspects. They were bad for business." He reminded us that we had signed up to work a detail the next day at the Pride parade. He said, "Make sure you guys' dress sexy tomorrow." We didn't know exactly what he meant but said that we would.

Chapter 4

June and I always signed up to work a lot of details. A detail was when a police officer was detailed outside of his district to provide additional manpower for ball games, parades, festivals, traffic, etc. We wanted to get a feel for what it felt like to work in other parts of the city. This Pride parade, which we knew nothing about, was on the North side of Chicago. We thought it would be a nice change of pace and a parade in the summer time sounded like a good idea.

We signed up to work details, and we also worked special employment, or special. When we worked a detail it was our regular tour duty, part of our 40 hour work week. Special employment was overtime. Most police officers had part-time jobs but if you worked special you made a police salary in oppose to what a private business might pay you. Some guys preferred part-time jobs that paid in cash.

Police officers who worked special employment either worked for the Chicago Transit Authority ("CTA") or for the Chicago housing Authority ("CHA"). When we worked for CTA we rode the buses and trains and provided the citizens with a sense of security. When we worked for CHA we assisted whatever district we were working in by answering calls in the housing projects. June and I signed up to work both of them from time to time but he didn't like working for CHA. I did. I was born in the projects and shared a kindred spirit with the people.

After working CTA a few times, we learned that the key to getting done quicker was by identifying the busiest routes, the routes that had the most buses run on it. And to get to roll call early and request that route. It was a first come, first serve basis. So after working for a few times we identified the busiest routes and the next time we worked CTA we would requested that route.

Roll call for special employment CTA was held at a substation on the north side of the city. The day I got to work June was already there. He was always very punctual and said, "We shouldn't have any problem getting our request today. I was the first person here and already handed the sergeant our requested route." Roll call was filling up fast and we were glad that we got there early. The sergeant came in, announced that roll call was starting and made some general announcements. When he was ending roll call, two white police officers came in late. The sergeant looked at them and we assumed that he marked them present. It was obvious that they all knew each other. He said, "Look at what the cat dragged in. Late again." One guy said, "If you hadn't insisted on buying one more round of drinks last night, we might've made it on time." They wrote down their request and handed it to the sergeant. When roll call was over the sergeant called out the routes. He read off the last officer's names first and gave them the route we requested. June and I looked at each other. Then he proceeded to give all the plum routes to all the white police officers. He looked at them, nodded for them to approach the podium and asked them which route they wanted. When he was finished with all the white officers, the only ones remaining were two Asian officers, a male and a female, June and me. When the sergeant dismissed roll call we went to confront him. June said, "Serge, I got here first and requested the route you gave to those white officers who came in last." The squat white sergeant said that they were there already and requested it before we did, which we knew was a lie. Then he said, in a snide, nasty manner, "Are you people gonna work or not?" That was the last time either one of us worked special for CTA.

June and I decided to ride to the north side together in one vehicle. We thought parking might be tight. He had the nicer truck and a tank full of gas. We met at the 9th district where I parked my car and jumped into his truck for the short ride to the northside. Roll call was at 8:00am and we didn't want to be late. We jumped on the Dan Ryan, then Lake Shore Drive, and onto the 23rd district on the north side of Chicago. Chicago was beautiful that time of morning. It was already warm and I knew it was going to be a hot day.

At roll call we got our assignments and we were assigned to a traffic detail. We weren't on the parade route but we were a block away from each other. The sergeant took care of us because he knew we were together. I guess all white folks ain't bad. He gave us our bright neon-colored vest and told us to be on our post at 11:00am. A guy who was in the academy with June was also there. His girl dropped him off so he jumped in the truck with us. He was a skinny, stringy-haired little white dude who was kind of aloof. We had a little time to kill so we went to breakfast at a really nice pancake house. The food was excellent and they gave us a nice discount on our bill. After that we drove around for a while waiting for the parade to start. We went by the parade route and saw the people lining up. They were very friendly, very cordial...very happy and gay. We went to a park on Lake Shore Drive to wait until it was time to be on our post.

June introduced my to his friend. "This is my little white buddy Tyrone. We call him Ty for short. How many white boys do you know named Tyrone? In the academy we called him Whitey because Ty backwards is Whitey." June nudged me and said, "Hey Whitey, how bout them Cubs?" Whitey looked up from his cell phone and said, "You know how feel about them losers. I hate them, and these sissies. They give me the creeps. I can't stand them!"

June said, "Why are you so hostile towards gay people. They are people just like us. There are gay people in my family and there are gay cops. I guess you just love who you love. We shouldn't be disrespecting anyone. I heard somewhere that we shouldn't judge anybody and only GOD can judge us."

I said, "JESUS said do not judge others and you will not be judged."

June turned to me and said, "I thought Tupac said that. Is that where he got it from?" I looked at him like he was crazy. I continued, "There is one thing I disagree with, people get a sex change. GOD made you what HE wanted you to be. HE don't make no mistakes."

June said, "Whitey was born and raised in Bridgeport and is a die-hard White Sox fan. Something tells me that all the good city jobs and services go to the people who live in Bridgeport."

Whitey was in the back seat of the truck and made a call. He was talking to someone and said, "I thought you said if I shaved it, you were gonna do that thing you do."

After the parade was over, we went to a 7-11 store to get some beer for the ride back to the south side. It was very expensive. When we go to Whitey's block we sat for a while and finished our beers. Whitey said,

You know what, you may be right. A majority of the people who live in this community are either retired city workers or presently work there" pointing out each house as he identified the people. He was already drunk and had loosened up by that time. And he wanted to get more beers. White boys love their beer. June said he had to drive too far and I needed him to take me to my car. I didn't want to be caught in Bridgeport after dark. I had a nice buzz but wanted something a little stronger so I bought me a drink to take home. I was going to enjoy the remaining day off that I had.

When I drank I remembered how I mistreated Savanna. I was guilt stricken. I was living with my sister because Savanna put me out. I wanted to call her and apologized again but she said that she had heard it all before. I knew I was wrong. I kept missing up and she kept taking me back. But this time it felt different. She was seeing someone else and it was eating me up. She was always open and honest with me. I couldn't take it. I had to get myself together or risk losing her forever. I had to go and talk to her but on this night, I wasn't going anywhere. I was drunk. I couldn't see or find my shoes. And I couldn't drive. I'd have to wait until tomorrow. That damn Crown Royal!

Chapter 5

Early the next morning my sister woke me up and asked me to go to Walgreens for her. It wasn't really that early, it was after 8:00am. I jumped up out of bed and grabbed the first shirt I saw and it just happened to be the same shirt I wore when I went out with June and Dorena. I was still hungover and couldn't remember if I brushed my teeth.

When we were kids my sister got a kick out of sending me to the store to get her sanitary products. She knew it embarrassed me to buy that stuff but she was older than me and I felt like I had to buy it. Another thing she did was send me to the store with a list of things to buy but she never gave me enough money and expected me to use my own money.

That morning When I walked into the store, I heard a commotion between the cashier and a customer at the cosmetic counter. A guy was being loud and profane and acting a fool. I turned back and stood a few feet away from them. He pushed a display from the counter to the floor and put his finger in her face. She slapped his hand away, he slapped her face and I jumped on his back. He tried to buck me off but I put him in a chokehold. We fought for what seemed like forever. I hit him and he hit the floor. I kept hitting him and he desperately fought back. Finally the police arrived but he wouldn't let us handcuff him. I had already identified myself as a police officer. Once we finally handcuffed him I noticed that his finger was dislocated. The store was a mess and there were people everywhere. One lady said, "Y'all didn't have to do that to him. That was excessive!" In my mind I thought lady you'd better get out of my face but I just looked at her like she was crazy. Even though I didn't always obey all the GODLY commands, decrees, and regulations that my grandmother taught me, I wasn't about to disrespect the woman who was old enough to be my mother. But I thought about it.

I was exhausted but still had to give my version of the story to the sergeant who was at the scene. At the end of the interview, he asked me had I been drinking. I told him I was at the Pride parade the day before and had a few drinks afterwards. He looked me up and down, then at my shirt, and said, "You don't look like one but who am I to judge. Next time don't celebrate too much." I think he was trying to hold his breath while talking to me. I guess I hadn't brushed my teeth.

Later that day I wanted to talk to Savanna and beg her to give me another chance. This would be my day of reckoning. I called her and asked her if I could come by. She was always pleasant to me even though I didn't always deserve it. I got myself together, brusher my teeth, and went to the house I still paid the mortgage on. When I pulled up, she was standing outside talking to her friend Edie who lived down the street with her sister. I heard that they were quite talented in the sack. Men gossip more than women do. Edie subtly tried to ask Savanna if she was going to Stooges that night but

Savanna wasn't going because she had already worked and went to class and she was tired. She went back to school to get her Master's degree. She was very independent and she let me know many times that she did not need a man in her life if he wasn't going to be right. When I got out of the car she hugged me and offered me a sip of her drink which I accepted. Crown Royal, a woman after my own heart. I had only been gone a couple of weeks but the house seemed quite different. We talked. I beg. She nodded and said, "You know what my favorite aphorism is- "we can get through anything together." But you seemed to only think about yourself. Let me tell you something, I'm not going to keep living like this. Either you are gonna get your shit together or I'm gone." She said a lot more and everything she said was right. I said I was done playing around, staying out late and arguing. I told her I'd cut back on drinking. I thought to myself, she drank, so I should be able to drink. Just like a nigga. I wanted to ask her if she was still seeing that guy but thought I'd leave on that positive note. When I told her I had even gone back to church, she guffawed. I knew she was serious this time. She said we'd talk more later because she worked all day and just got out of class.

    I left feeling better. I sat in the car basking because of how good the meeting went. I should have been satisfied with that and left well enough alone. Then I remembered that Edie tried to sneak a question to Savanna when I pulled up, asking her if she was going to Stooges. Stooges was a local bar, probably where Savanna and her paramour hung out. Since Savanna wasn't going, I thought maybe I'd go, just to see what I could see. I don't know why I wanted to go. I don't know what I was looking for. The cop in me felt like I needed to check something out for myself. I should have taken my ass home that night but I went anyway.

CHAPTER 6

When I got to Stooges there were only three people there, the bartender and two older men, neither of which seemed to be Savanna's type. I knew her former boyfriend so I knew her type. The lounge was dimly lit. There was a long bar on one side, and tables and bar stools on the wall. The jukebox had some nice jazz CD's inside. I sat at the bar a little ways away from the two older men. Cops are nosey so I kept my ears open. I only ordered beer, even though the Crown Royal looked good because I wanted to be sharp to hear whatever it was I went there to listen for. I smoked a cigarette and waited.

After few minutes two guys came in. When the bartender saw them coming she poured their drinks. They were obviously regulars. They sat at a table right behind me. One guy nodded at me when he came to the bar, grabbed their drinks and went to their table. They immediately started talking about drug transactions and they weren't discreet. Being a cop I understood the vernacular and knew these weren't the guys I was "looking" for. Surely my wife wouldn't be dating a drug dealer. I walked over to the jukebox and saw some music Savanna and I really liked, some early Luther Vandross songs. I wondered if Savanna played any of those songs for her friend when they were there. I played 'The Weasil' a song by Donald Byrd that I liked. When I returned to my seat they had switched from talking about drugs and were now talking about a married woman that the light-skinned one was dating. He said he had to be extra careful because he thought that her husband might be a cop. I almost choked on my cigarette. I ordered another beer and tuned in. Again these guys weren't discreet at all in fact they seemed to relish the fact that he was dating a policeman's wife. They laughed and joked until the big guy had to use the bathroom. I looked at the other guy through the mirror, the one who was bragging, and knew I'd never forget that face. When his friend came back, he stood up the leave. The big guy walked over to the bartender, pulled out a wad of money and gave her a generous tip. They headed for the door and I got up too. They stopped to talk to the two older men who were seated at the bar. I maneuvered around them and went outside. I stood outside and pulled my phone out like I was making a call. A few seconds later they came out and got into the rimmed-up Ford Expedition that was parked right in front of the bar. I walked to the back of the truck like I was making a call and memorized the license plates. When they pulled off, I wrote the numbers down on a scratch sheet of paper. I don't know what this was, maybe something, maybe nothing.

A few days later while I was a work, I ran the license plates to the truck. It was registered to a young woman who lived a few blocks from Savanna's house. I remembered a nickname of one of the guy's and found a mug-shot that matched the guy who was there. Then I ran his name and got a list of people he was associated with and arrested with. The CPD had a database with all kinds of information. A name came back to someone who lived at the same address of the young woman where the truck was registered. I was doing some serious police work for all the wrong reasons.

The big guy who had the wad of money and paid for the drinks, his nickname was Turtle. The other guy was Jasper. The truck was registered to a woman who lived at Jasper's address. Was this the information that I was looking for? Turtle didn't appear to be Savanna's type but Jasper did. I think I knew my wife's type. Was I a pissed-off, jealous, insecure husband? Probably. I don't know why I had it in for the guy. Men are only doing what men do. He can only get as far as the woman lets him. I don't know if my wife was the one this guy was bragging about sleeping with. Something told me he was even though I wasn't sure. I stared at his mug shot with contempt and thought to myself, light-skinned niggas think they shit don't stink!

One evening that Crown Royal told me to drive by Jasper's house just to see what I could see. Then I drove by there regularly to see if Savanna's car was ever there but it never was. I did see his truck out there. Once as I was driving by, I saw a guy parked in a van also watching the house. I went around the block and parked several cars behind him. When he looked in his mirror and saw me he pulled off. I only caught a glimpse of him. He looked like a cop I knew named Yunus. He had a reputation for having a short temper and a bad attitude. A few minutes later I saw Savanna drive by but she didn't see me nor did she stop. I was about to leave when I saw Jasper and a young lady come from inside the house. He walked her to her car, hugged and kissed her and smacked her on her fat ass. She looked very happy and very satisfied. She got into her car and drove away. Jasper got into another car and drove away too.

Chapter 7

One day I saw Jasper's truck in the parking lot of the liquor store. I did a U-turn and drove into the parking lot. I was walking into the store as he was coming out. I walked right in front of him, blocking his way, and said, "I gonna say this one time and I'm never going to say it again, stay away from my wife." His eyes got big. he didn't ask me who I was or who my wife was. He didn't say anything. He just stepped around me and walked away.

In addition to selling weed, Jasper also owned a beauty shop and some property. People often bought him things to buy, sell, and trade. He was messing around with several women, one he knew was married to a policeman. He had never seen me prior to our brief meeting. Turtle was his callow right hand man, his security, and his drop-off man. Once a week Turtle went out to the projects for Jasper to either drop something off for him or pick something up. He claims to never really know what he was dropping off. He trusted Jasper. When he got out there he met a guy he always did business with. Turtle didn't drink or smoke before the drop-offs. And he knew to make sure he had his driver's license. Turtle also knew that the registration and insurance card were over the visor. On the day of the drop-off Jasper would put the bag on the floor on the back seat, turn on the car and return back into the house where he'd stand in the window and wait for Turtle. Turtle walked the short distance from his house and got into the car for the drive out to the projects. They had done these runs many times before and had them down pat.

On the night before a drop-off Turtle's cousin came by his house and brought some weed, alcohol, and females to celebrate him getting out of Cook County. They drank and smoked until early in the morning. Turtle got up on time the next morning and got ready to go to Jasper's. He told his cousin, who was still sleeping, that he'd back in a little while. He hit the blunt that was in the ashtray one time before he left. He made sure he had his driver's license and left for Jasper's house. Jasper could see Turtle once he hit the block. Turtle nodded to him, got into the car and drove away. When he got about a block away he lit a cigarette and it boosted his high. Then he remembered that the night before they smoked primos, marijuana laced with cocaine and the blunt that was in the ashtray was one from last night. He turned the music up really loud when a song he liked came on. His usual route was to go to South Chicago Ave. turn right onto 79th and Stony Island, and on to the projects. He had driven the route many times before and usually didn't deviate from his route, but on this day the smell of White Castles hit him and since he had the munchies he went into the drive through and ordered himself 10 cheeseburgers, an order of onion rings, a large french fries and a vanilla shake. When he was passing Kenwood Liquor store he saw some fine women coming out and had to swerve to avoid hitting a car. A police woman saw his reckless driving and curbed him. She got out of her car and approached his car. When she got close to the door he pulled off and sped away. He looked in the rearview mirror to see where she was and slammed into the back of a semi-trailer truck.

Turtle woke up at the police station when he heard someone popping their gum. He was handcuffed to the wall, he didn't have any shoes on and his head was throbbing. The police asked him if he needed medical attention. The lady police officer had his driver's license and was sitting at the table writing something. Turtle had his head in his hands not knowing what to do. He was nervous and scared because he didn't know exactly what was in the bag. One time when he did a drop-off, the guy wanted to verify that what was suppose to be in the bag was actually in there. When he opened it, it contained several pounds of marijuana, a half a bird, a gun and some money. He remembered some of the horror stories that his cousin had shared with him about what went on at Cook County and he didn't want any parts of that life. He couldn't think straight and he looked around and blurted out, "Hey, where's my bag?" The officers looked at each other and said, "We don't know, give us your keys and we'll check the car." The keys were on the table with the rest of Turtle's property and without thinking he slid the keys to them. He wasn't bright and he was kind of slow. I think that's why they called him Turtle. One officer said, "Why did you try to run? If you have some information that can help you get out of this situation now is the time to give it up." Turtle said, "I'm scared of the police. Y'all shoot people!" The police officer looked and pointed at the female police officer and said, "You're scared of her?" Turtle put his head back in his hand and started talking. He told them where he was going and what he was about to do. He told them who he worked for. He talked to them for about an hour and gave them a lot of valuable information. When he was almost finished, he remembered one more thing. He told them that Jasper was messing around with a policeman's wife and he thinks that the cop threatened him. Turtle said that they listened to him but didn't seem that interested. He said that one day he was outside his house when a big dude confronted him. "This big dude came up to me and called me by my government name. He knew everything about me, my mother's name, my baby-mama's name, everything. He knew everybody who lived in my house. Then he started asking me questions about Jasper. He also knew everything about him. I know he was a cop because of the kinds of questions he asked. He made me nervous. He was a big, bad, scary dude." Turtle asked them what they were going to do about it but felt like they weren't going to do anything. He was frustrated because he couldn't describe the guy, probably because he was always high or drunk when he saw him.

The officer returned with the bag and walked it over to Turtle. He asked Turtle if he knew what was in the bag but Turtle didn't say anything. They gathered around the bag, looked inside and looked at Turtle. He dropped his head. One of them said, "Well, well, well, look at what we have here." He pulled out several small bags of marijuana and three brand new pairs of Timberland boots. The female police officer walked over to him and handed him the traffic tickets she was writing. She said, "Why'd you run? I was just going to make sure you had your driver's license and proof of insurance and then let you go. I wasn't going to write you any tickets, I hate writing tickets. But since you tried to run and crashed into the back of that truck, I had no other choice but to fill out an accident report and write you some tickets. Now your dumbass is getting locked up for possessing marijuana, drugs that we never would have found if you hadn't told us about it." She continued, "Look here suga, get out of the drugs selling business. You're not good at it. You're either going to wind up in prison or dead. That life is not for you. I've seen it many times before." She shook her head and walked away. The other police officer said, "Thanks for the information. We'll be looking into that information real soon." And off he went to the lockup.

Chapter 8

One evening after roll call June and I were standing around waiting for a phone to become available. We both had mobile phones which weren't as ubiquitous as they are now. The plans we had with our cell phone providers only limited us to a couple of hundred minutes per month so we saved our minutes and used the telephones at the police station a lot. Our sergeant walked up to me and told me that I had to report directly to the medical section at the police academy to submit a sample of my urine. They usually notified you immediately after roll that you were randomly chosen for a drug test which only allotted you a limited amount of time to get there. Aside from being randomly chosen, the other times you had to submit urine for drug test was if you discharged your weapon, was suspected of drug use, or was charged with a crime and arrested. Officers who had drugs in their system sometimes tried to take remedies to try and flush their systems before the tests. To my knowledge nothing ever worked and if illegal drugs were found in your system you'd be fired. Even though I didn't use drugs it made me nervous whenever I had to take a test. Now if they screened for excessive amounts of alcohol in your system, they would've had me. I drank a lot in those days.

Since June was my partner, he'd ride to the academy with me but he didn't have to give a sample of his pee. We enjoyed leaving our district for any myriad reasons. There were many good restaurants to eat in in our district but so many more outside of our district and on this trip, we would surely take advantage of this opportunity. Wherever we wanted to eat had to be in the vicinity of the police academy so MacArthur's, the best soul food restaurant in the city, was too far away. On this day we decided to go to Al's Beef on Taylor Street for an Italian combo, also, the best in the city.

When we got to the academy, we saw a young Hispanic female police officer that June knew. She was assigned there as an instructor. He stopped to talk to her while I continued on to the medical section. I had only recently graduated from the academy, maybe a little more than a year, but it seemed quite different. It was late in the afternoon but some recruits, or probationary police officers (PPO's) were still there. Some where in study groups and others were running and working out in the gym. This was part of the future of Chicago's police department, young people excited at the prospect of serving and protecting the citizens of Chicago. I reported to the medical section and the sergeant who was on duty. There were several other police officers also waiting to provide samples of their urine. Some of them looked as nervous as I did.

Every police officer knows if they can pass the piss test, as it's commonly called, before they take it. If they know they'll fail the test they'll go through extreme measures to try and pass, even by getting their partner's pee. I once heard that an officer paid his partner for his pee. They stopped at Walgreens on the way to the academy and bought a pack of condoms or balloons and the partner peed in the condom/balloon. The officer then gave his partner his pee and the officer took it into the bathroom/exam room of the academy to pass it off as his own. The medical staff or sergeant accompanies the officer into the bathroom or exam room while you're peeing to make sure that the sample that you're providing is in fact your own pee. They usually stood halfway in the room with you with the door open. It takes precision, patience, and a steady hand to get that pee from that condom/balloon into that sample cup without wasting any on your hand.

When I was done submitting my sample, I gave it to the medical staff who attached my signature from a prepared card to the sample and whisked it away. He was very cavalier with my pee. I was a little nervous and may have missed the cup a bit but it was cool because it was my own pee. I washed my hands and went to look for June. Before I left, I asked the sergeant on duty when I might know the results of my test. He looked at me over the top of his glasses and said, "If you piss hot, you'll know soon enough." When I found June he was laughing and joking with the young Boricua.

I had a lazy habit of referring to all Hispanics as Mexicans even though June told me to stop doing that. He tried to describe the differences in features among Hispanics but I got weary of trying. They all looked the same to me. As I approached them she looked at me and switched from speaking English to speak in Spanish. June also looked at me but he had a dumbass confused look on his face. He was born in the United States and didn't speak Spanish although he claimed to know some of it. He gesticulated a hand washing gesture at me and said, "Did you wash your hands already?

Are you ready to go?" He was a germaphobe like I was. Before I answered, he turned his attention back to the senorita and concluded their conversation. While walking back to our car, he lit a cigarette and said, "Was there soap in the bathroom to wash your hands with?" I said, "When you were here, was there ever soap in the bathrooms?" He said, "No, that's why I always carried a small bottle of hand soap with me everyday. And you didn't answer my question. Was there soap in the bathroom for you to wash your hands with?" He stood on the driver's side of the car with the keys in his hand staring at me, waiting for me to answer his question before he opened the door. We stared at each other for a few seconds and I said, "yeah, I washed my hands with the soap now open this fucking door!" When I got in the car I said, "Whenever you have a piss test, you don't have to touch anybody else's... thing. Mines is clean. I know where it's been, it's been with me all day. He looked at me and sped out of the parking space. We went to Al's Beef and enjoyed our lunch.

When we got back to our district, we notified our sergeant via the radio that we were back. We also notified the dispatcher that we were available for any jobs she had. I said to June, "I noticed that when I approached you and the senorita at the academy you guys were talking in English but she switched to Spanish mid-sentence when she saw me. What was up with that? What was she saying that she felt the need to switch to speak you in Spanish? Does she know that you don't speak Spanish? That's why you had that dumbass look on your face. You didn't know what she was saying either. Did you?" He said, "I don't speak it but there are some things I understand." The dispatcher called us and said, "I got a job for you guys. It's an old call, maybe 30 minutes old, but I need you to check on a suspicious car playing loud music in the school parking lot. The caller said that there are several male blacks in a 4-door brown sedan in the faculty parking lot of Chicago Vocational high school. Like I said this call come in about 30 minutes ago so the car might be gone but I gotta send someone anyway. Check it out and let me know. The school's been closed for several hours already." We said we'd check it out.

Chicago Vocational High School is a huge school in the heart of an area of the city where middle class black folks live. The homeowners worked hard, took care of their property and neighborhood and deserved high quality police service. We were only a few blocks away from the school and came in from the back. When the guys looked in their mirrors and saw us, they turned the music down and sat up in their reclined seats. On the ground outside the car on the passenger's side was a brown paper bag with empty cans of Old English Malt Liquor, wrappers from a fast-food restaurant and cigarette butts. We exited our car and approached theirs. Two guys were in the front seats, and one guy was in the back. All young guys but only a few years younger than June and I. June motioned for the driver to roll down his window. The passenger and the guy in the back both looked over their right shoulders at me. I motioned for the front seat passenger to roll down his window. I said, "Do me a favor, little brother, and put your hands where I can see them." The front seat passenger slowly put his hands on the dashboard. The guy in the back quickly threw his hands up. I heard June ask the driver for his license. The guy respectfully said, "Sir, I don't have my license. I have a ticket." June opened the door and told the guy to step out, all the while positioning himself so the guy could not break and run. He turned the guy to face the car, patted him down, and put handcuffs on him. Then he took him to our car. He came back and got the front seat passenger out and did the same thing to him. When he got that guy in our car, I got the last guy out, handcuffed him, patted him down and took him to the rear of their car. June searched the car and the guy said, "Officer, all we got is some Old E and a little weed." After June searched the car, he went back to talk to the other guys that were in our backseat to run all their names and the car's vehicle identification number. The car came back registered to the person he described, his baby's-mama's mama. After June ran their names, I asked them why they were disrespecting the people on the block by playing loud music and throwing trash on the streets. "Y'all do stupid shit to attract attention to yourselves, and y'all driving without a driver's license. And you wonder why the police are always messing with you. How would you feel if somebody was sitting on your block playing loud music and throwing trash on the ground?" The front seat passenger said, "I'd mind my own business. And with all due respect, officer, we weren't driving. The car is parked." I said, "That's because you don't own shit. This guy was in the driver's seat with the keys in the ignition. The car didn't get here by itself. So that means he is in control of the car and is responsible for it, its passengers, and the contents of the car, smart ass." The driver looked at his friend and said, "Cool out Malik, I got this." He looked at us earnestly and said, "I know we're wrong officer and we're sorry but all we got is a little bud and some Old E. We ain't got no guns or no warrants or nothing like that. If you give us a break we're outta here." June said, "Y'all can't drive this car because you been drinking and getting high and you ain't got no driver's license." I asked them where they got the weed from and the back seat passenger said from the Mexicans on the east side. June said, "Are you sure they are

Mexicans or are you calling them that because they look Hispanic?" The guy said, "What?" I looked at June and said, "What's up? What are we gonna do with these guys?" They looked at June with doleful eyes. I had worked with June long enough to know what we were going to do with them. We weren't going to waste our time. It wasn't a big deal to us. We learned to use our discretion when it came to making arrests. A veteran officer told us to make a lot of arrests and learn how to do the paperwork correctly. That also meant making a lot of frivolous arrests. Sometimes when we made arrests and went to court the State's Attorney would ask us what we wanted to do as far as a seeking conviction or not. They'd ask if the arrestee was belligerent or remorseful and they'd leave the decision to us. We were young and inexperienced and didn't know what to do so we asked them for their advice. Most times they'd tell us that it wasn't a serious offense and if it was okay with us they were going to nolle-pros it. Other officers told us to try and only target quality arrests and this was definitely not a high-quality arrest. Even though we weren't going to arrest them that didn't stop me from asking where they got the weed from. The passenger repeated himself and said it was the Mexicans who were on the east side. Like I knew who 'the' Mexicans were. I said, "That's all you got? No descriptions or addresses? He said," Officer, for them, it's only snitching if they tell on each other. But I can't tell on them. Plus I don't have any more information because that's all I know. If we want some weed we beep them and they meet us somewhere on the east side. If they found out we snitched they'd cut us off. They got the best deals on weed since the police shut down the Shalom Homes. But if you want to know what they look like, one of them looks just like him" and he pointed at June. June said, "Are you insinuating that I'm Mexican?" The guy said, "You are, ain't you?" I looked at June and snickered. June looked at him, huffed and rolled his eyes, then he looked back at me and went to take the handcuffs off the guys. The guy said, "What's wrong with him?" I said you insulted him by implying that he was a Mexican. He said, "I didn't mean no disrespect. They all look the same to me." June told them that they'd have to leave the car and and come back with a licensed driver since none of them had driver's license. One guy asked us if we could drive the car to their house. I said, "If I drive it anywhere it's gonna be to the police station and confiscate it with you guys as arrestees. You still want me to drive it in?" They quickly changed their minds. One guy said, "How are we suppose to get to the crib? We can't walk in this neighborhood. These guys don't know us." I said can't you call someone to come and pick you up? Does anybody have a cell phone? They said no. June asked them if they wanted us to drop them off somewhere and they all looked at each other and said yeah. I told them to pick up the trash they threw on the ground and put it in the trash can that was only about 20ft away. They also made sure all the doors to the car were locked. I took their weed and threw it on the ground and smashed it with my foot. They gasped for air, dropped and nodded their heads but didn't say anything. I patted each one of them down again before they got into our car. I placed the keys to the car into the driver's hand and they giggled like silly kids when they climbed into the back of our car. June asked them where they wanted to go and they pointed south. The driver said, "Y'all can just drop us of at the White Castle's on 95th street." When we got to the White Castles they looked around nervously before they quickly exited our car. Some young ladies they knew were coming out of the restaurant and I said, "Hey fellas, I'll holla at y'all later." They didn't turn around or acknowledge us nor did they think that was funny. I checked the backseat of our car to make sure they didn't leave any weed back there. That would not be our last encounter with those guys especially the young contentious Malik.

We told the dispatcher that we were clear, then we drove to the 7-11 on 87th street to get coffee. We no longer patronized the Dunkin Donuts in our district because of something that happened several weeks ago. One time we went there for coffee and they gave us a cup for half price. It was always nice when the businesses looked out for us, we appreciated it and thought it was nice of them. As we stood there putting cream and sugar in our coffee, two white police officers came in to get coffee. We watched as the cashier gave them two cups of coffee but didn't charge them anything. June was friendlier with them than I was and asked them about it. The officer said that as far as he knew they gave all police officers a free cup of coffee. June and I immediately accused them of being racists and never went back. One day there was a call of a disturbance at the Dunkin Donuts. Since we were only a few blocks away we told the dispatcher that we'd handle the job. When we got there the manager told us a homeless man was disturbing the customers and wanted him to leave. We explained to the man that the manager didn't want him on the property and he left. The manager offered us a cup of coffee but we declined it.

While we were on our way to the 7-11 our sergeant called and requested to meet with us. I told him that we were on our way to the 7-11 and he told us that he'd meet us there. When we came out he was pulling up. He said, "I don't know exactly what's going on with you" pointing to me "but you've been reassigned pending an investigation." June and I looked at each other and said, "What!?" "You need to report directly to the watch commander right now." We jumped into our car and sped to the station. Instantly I got nervous and felt like I had to use the bathroom. June said," Do you think you failed the drug test?" I looked at him and nodded no. A few minutes later he said, "Do you smoke reefer?" I looked at him like he was crazy. A few minutes after that, he said, "Cocaine? Do you do a line or two on your days off?" I said, "Hell no June, you know I don't do drugs. What's the matter with you?" He said, "Something's going on with you. A couple hours after you take a drug test, they are pulling you off the streets. Something ain't right." I lit a cigarette but didn't say anything.

I went straight to the watch commander's office when I got to the station and June was right with me. His secretary's desk was right outside his office and she waved me in when she saw me coming. She already knew what was going on and was waiting for me but told June's nosey ass that he couldn't go in so he went to use the telephone. She knocked on his door and walked in without being invited in. A few seconds later she came out, leaves the door open, and tells me to go inside. I walked in and the lieutenant turned down his music, Bob James and David Sanborns' Double Vision's cassette was on the table. He was also an Irish lieutenant but he was more laidback and reserved. He had a napkin tucked into his shirt and covered his food but not before I saw what he was eating; smothered pork chops, macaroni and cheese, dressing, collard greens, sweet potatoes, cole slaw, and a diet Pepsi. I wanted to ask him where he got it from because it smelled really good. I said, "I'm sorry lieu-- I didn't mean to interrupt your lunch but the sergeant told me to report directly to you. I can come back later." He stopped chewing his food long enough to say, "No, this is important. You are hereby formally notified that effective immediately the Internal Affairs' Division has launched a formal investigation against you. You are to report to the callback unit tomorrow morning at 0800 hours. That's all I'm gonna tell you. The sergeant down there will brief you on the complaint. So take the rest of the night off, go on home and try to get a good night's sleep. When you go down there do not take your weapon, only carry your identification card with you. You won't have any official police powers until the investigation is completed and you've been cleared to return to full duty. Do not consume excessive amounts of alcohol." I was screwed! "Sometimes these things are serious, sometimes they come out to be nothing. Try not to worry about it. I know that's easy for me to say, I'm not being investigated by IAD. Make sure you're on time tomorrow." He asked me if I knew where the callback unit was and I told him I did not know where it was. He said his secretary would give me the address. He said, "I know you got a lot of questions but wait until tomorrow and let the sergeant fill you in." I left his office and went to update June on what he told me. June had as many questions as I had. I told him I was leaving and I'd call him when I got off work tomorrow. I was in a daze as I changed clothes and drove home. I also called Savanna and told her what happened. Don't drink alcohol in excess-- he must've been crazy!

When I got home, I had a shot of Crown Royal and a beer. My sister asked me why I was home so early and I explained it to her. I didn't have a problem falling asleep or staying asleep. I woke up extra early to make sure I'd be on time. No longer could I roll out of bed 45 minutes before roll call and make it to work on time. Now I had to make the hour plus trek to a gentrified section of the west side of Chicago. And I made sure to brush my teeth. Twice.

Chapter 9

When I got to the callback unit a pregnant black police officer escorted me into the lunchroom where I was to sit and wait for the sergeant who was on duty. After a few minutes the sergeant came in with a manila folder and extended his hand to shake. I thought to myself this can't be too bad if the sergeant wants to shake my hand. He introduced himself to me, he was Sergeant Kelly, one of many Chicago police sergeants assigned there, and he told me why I was there. "The Internal Affairs Division has launched an investigation alleging that you used excessive force against a federal employee. He said that you used unauthorized chokehold on him, you used a racial slur and that you were drunk. He said you called him a nigger." The sergeant said nigger, not the N-word, or nigga, He said nigger, and I think he got a kick out of it. He also said that I was the one who broke his finger. "Do you remember this incident that occurred at a Walgreens?" I said I did. He continued, "He said he was talking to a cashier, discussing a matter, when out of the blue you walked up to him and hit him for no reason." I tried to offer a defense but he said now was not the time and that it would come later. The complainant failed to mention that he was loud, profane, and that he assaulted the cashier. In the meanwhile I would be assigned there to work from Saturday to Wednesday, 0800-1600hrs. I would answer the telephone, take calls of non-emergencies, and fill out reports. I was to not drink alcohol in excess, whatever the hell that meant, and to keep a clear conduct. What he said was partially true. I wasn't drunk. I may have been slightly hungover. I did call him a nigga. I said, "Stop resisting nigga!" I was still a sworn police officer but until the investigation was completed, I wouldn't have any police powers. I couldn't carry my gun. I couldn't make arrests or work overtime. If I walked into a Walgreens and somebody was being belligerent, I wasn't suppose to intervene. I was suppose to get a good description of the person and their vehicle if he had one, and call the police. Don't be a hero!

This is where the Chicago police officers who were stripped of their duty went when they were put on administrative leave and investigated for misconduct. It didn't take long for me to get acclimated to my new position. When I first arrived there I was embarrassed that as a police officer I would be investigated for misconduct, that is until I found out why other police officers were there. My offense paled in comparison to what other officers were accused of. It wasn't a big secret why we were there. These were still police officers and they were nosey by nature. Everybody knew everybody else's business. Some police officers were there for domestics with their spouses. Some officers had gotten DUIs. Others had discharged their weapons or had drugs in their systems. And there were several pregnant police officers there. We would be there until our investigation was completed, or until the pregnant officers had their babies. I'm just glad excessive consumption of alcohol wasn't a punishable offense. If it was there wouldn't be enough police officers to patrol the streets of Chicago.

After a couple of weeks of being there the sergeant told me that during the investigation, they found someone who witnessed the entire incident and spoke up for me on my behalf. He said that it was a good sign. However, a camera did show that I used a forbidden chokehold on the guy.

There was a white police officer who was being investigated for shooting an unarmed black teen in the back. Supposedly a gun was recovered from the scene. There was also a rumor that the city offered the family a minuscule cash settlement and a house in the suburbs in exchange for them not suing the city and the family accepted it. Soon after that the officer was cleared to return to work but he was reassigned to a cushy spot outside of the patrol division.

One day I was in the break room drinking coffee and there were two policewomen sitting at a nearby table. One of them was very pregnant and looked like she was going to drop that kid any minute. The other one was under investigation for having marijuana in her system. She argued that marijuana was harmless and should be legal. She was right but it was still illegal. The pregnant police officer said something that struck a nerve. Talking to the other women she said, "My husband is a good man, a good father, and a good provider but he doesn't satisfy me sexually." Her admission took me back to the time when June told me that Savanna might want to leave me because she liked being with her paramour.

While at the callback unit I saw how the Chicago Police department disciplined its officers. As for the police officer who shot and killed the teenager, what he did affected him, his family, the victim's family, and the police department's relationship with the community. But he was still going to be a police officer. The woman who had marijuana in her system was going to be relieved of her duty as a police officer and fired. Her selfish act would only affect her and her family's livelihood. Something was very wrong with that picture. I don't know if I was ever at risk of losing my job because of the investigation but you never know, light-skinned people had a lot of clout in those days. They really thought their shit didn't stink.

Chapter 10

On one of my days off June called and said he wanted to come by and check up on me. He wanted to see how I was doing and that he needed to talk to me about something important. He was working by himself and would spend his lunch with me. He seemed kind of glum and melancholy when I saw him. It felt like he had to force himself to smile. We stood outside and talked because it was a nice day. He said, "What is this place where your sister lives?" I said, "This is London Towne. It's really quiet out here. A lot of professional people live out here, several cops, firemen, teachers, lawyers, business owners, members of the clergy. It's really nice out here." He asked me if any Puerto Ricans lived out there. I told him I didn't know and that I'd find out. I explained what I did at the callback unit. I asked him how his days were and he told me what his days consisted of. He told me that the Latin guy we arrested in the Shalom's accused us of taking his money and he looked at me with furrowed eyebrows. I reminded him that it was him and the sergeant who counted the money while I did the other paperwork. He said, "What the hell was he doing with all that money anyway?" He continued, "One night the guys at work asked me to go out drinking with them and when I walked into the bar, I knew I had made a mistake. One cop immediately started talking about y'all. I think they're infatuated with black people because that's all they talk about. They don't have anything good to say about the brothers but they love black women. One guy said that Mexicans never would have tolerated slavery all those years and that Black people were weak. I looked at him like he was crazy, had one drink and left. I hate them niggas!" June asked me had I seen Savanna and I told him I did. I told him that I finally asked her if she was still seeing that dude and she said she wasn't. He said, "That's great. I hope you guys get back together soon. Y'all make a great couple."

June said after he left the bar, he called Dorena at work and told her he was going to stop by to see her before he went home. He said, "When I walked in she was laughing and joking with these two niggas at the end of the bar. I instantly got a pit in my stomach. She hugged and kissed me and seemed happy to see me. I sat down with the intention of having one drink and leaving but my attention was mostly on those guys. I know that part of her job is interacting with the customers but something told me that they were there for more than drinks and chicken wings. I was so insecure that I sat there until she got off at 2am. This woman has got me going crazy. She's clearly out of my league. I really like her and I want to be with her but how can I trust her working in that environment? I can't get her out of my system. Sometimes I feel like I'm in over my head with this woman- with this job. Anybody can accuse us of stealing money, or in your case, using excessive force." I said, "June, you gotta go and talk to her. Let her know how you feel. And be straight up with her. If you feel like something ain't right, then something ain't right. I know you want her all to yourself and you don't want to share her with anybody else, but whatcha gonna do? Sit up there every night? You can't be with her 24/7. You're gonna go crazy. And if she wants to have sex with someone, she's gonna do it. Either you're gonna trust her or you gotta leave her alone. I can't tell you what to do but what do you expect? She's young, fine, with a nice body, and serving drinks all night to horny ass dudes looking for a victim to take home. I'm sure guys are hitting on her every night. And think about this, you're taking advice from a guy who's suspended pending an investigation for being drunk and using excessive force." That made him smile.

He stared into space and changed the subject. "I wish you'd hurry and come back. How long are you going to be down there anyway?" I hunched my shoulders signaling that I didn't know. He said, "I was talking to a friend of mines and she told me that she worked in the 17th district, and working there or the 16th or 18th districts would be better than working here. I was thinking about transferring some place closer to home." I said, "Does Dorena know about this friend you talk to?" We talked some more then he asked if he could use the bathroom. I thought about my friend and all that he was going through. He sure took a long time in there. I think he did the number two in my sister's bathroom.

Chapter 11

Savanna called to tell me that she was barbequing and inviting me over. She was a great cook and knew I loved her cooking. She liked watching me devour her food. She gave me a list of things to bring, pop, alcohol, and ice. I got dressed, brushed my teeth and went to Indiana to get some gas and cigarettes. They were cheaper in Indiana and it was only a short drive from the house. On the way back I stopped at Kenwood Liquor store and bought some liquor and beer. I was so excited about the invitation to dinner and the fact that she was no longer seeing that guy anymore that I offered to take Savanna's car and fill it up with gas too. So I dropped off my car, the beer and alcohol, and picked up her car. I also washed her car. It was filthy. For her to claim that she didn't need a man to take care of her, I wondered why nobody washed that nasty ass car, but I digress. When I got back, and as I pulled up to the house, I saw two detectives going to the house. I could tell they were detectives by the cheap suits they had on. I couldn't imagine what they were there for. I wondered if they were there to check up on me, to see if I had been consuming excessive amounts of alcohol. A few hours later and I'd been in trouble.

Savanna's friend Edie opened the door for them. I was several feet behind them and walked in before the door closed. The two detectives, Pritt and Jeff, turned to look at me. Jeff and I frequented the same cop bar and played in the same police basketball league. He was perplexed to see me. He asked me if I lived there and I briefly explained the complicated arrangements. He answered with a drawn out, "Um-okay." Knowing detectives and how they operate, I knew the good cop/bad routine would be in play. Then he told us why they were there. Detective Pritt asked Savanna if she wanted to talk in private but she said it wasn't necessary. He asked her if she knew Jasper Knox and she said she did. Again, he asked her if she wanted to talk in private and again she said she did not. He asked her how she knew him and she said they dated briefly when she and I were separated. She said she ended it when she found out he had other women and did things she didn't approve of. He asked her if she knew he sold drugs. She looked down, nodded that she did then looked at me. Both detectives also looked at me. I asked them what this was all about and Pritt said, "Somebody caught Knox outside his house and beat him up pretty bad. His daughter heard a commotion outside their house, went to open the door and saw someone straddling her father and holding a gun on him. When she yelled at him, he pointed the gun at her. She said she ran back into the house to call the police. When she went by the window, she saw the guy running away. She didn't recognize him and never seen him before. The responding officers asked her was she home alone and she said she was. A neighbor was on her porch, said she knew the family and asked if she could help. The daughter said that several days ago she overheard her father talking to his friend and he said that a man threatened him in a liquor store parking lot. He said he thought the man was the husband of a woman he was having an affair with and that he might be a cop. We asked her if she knew of any of her father's girlfriends and the only person, she could think of was Savanna. She got Savanna's telephone number from Knox's phone book, we called Savanna and asked her could we come and talk to her, and here we are. He's in pretty bad shape. Who ever did it must've really had it in for him. There was a lot of blood everywhere." Savanna covered her mouth with her hands and looked at me. I was stoic. "The only description she had was that of a tall baldheaded black man running from the scene." Again they all looked at me probably because I "fit the description." I said, "You said he sold drugs. Maybe somebody tried to rob him during a transaction, or it was a rival dealer." Pritt turned to his partner, tilted his head towards me and said, "Thinking like a cop. No, we thought that too but he still had a pocket full of money, several bags of marijuana, his cell phone and car keys with him. Naw, this was personal." I said, "So why do you want to talk to Savanna? Do you think she had something to do with it?" "Our sergeant told us to check it out, this cop's wife angle." Pritt directed his next inquires to me. "What about you? Know anything? You know how this goes. When looking for the outlaws we start with the in-laws, those closest to the victim, and I'll use the term victim loosely. This thing, this attack, was done neatly, viciously, but neat. It was done by someone who knew what they were doing. A cop could probably do this thing and get away with it. And the jealous husband narrative fits perfectly into this story." Jeff interrupted, "What's up with your case with the guy from Walgreens?" Pritt interjected-- "That was you? I heard about that case. You're the cop who beat the shit out of the cop from the feds? I heard that was a brutal beating too. That one is reminiscent of this one." Now I could feel him about to try and get under my skin. "I can imagine that it pissed you off when you found out that some punk was nailing your wife." He kept referring to Savanna as Jasper's girlfriend and he was doing it on purpose. I said, "You keep referring to her as his girlfriend, she's not his girlfriend." Pritt said, "Call it what you want but you know what I mean. There was no real evidence left on the scene. Investigations like this won't last. We'll start it but we probably won't finish it. Something else will come along. Something more important. This is a big city and a lot goes on around here. You know we don't waste our valuable resources on a guy like this. I'm not so sure how much energy we'll put into finding the perp. If it was a jealous husband who got this guy, he probably deserved it. I know I'd be pissed if it were me. This ain't TV where we dedicate an entire episode to finding the offender in this case. You know it matters who the victim is, and this guy ain't much of a victim." Jeff said, "You smoke cigarettes? Newport's, right?" I said, "Yeah I smoke why?" He said, "While canvassing the area around the house we came across quite a few Newport cigarettes butts and it looked like someone was casing Knox." I smoked Newport Lights but I didn't say anything. I knew the answer to this next question but I asked it anyway. "Did you guys recover any of those butts to check for DNA?" Pritt looked over the top of his glasses and said, "Check for DNA? Are you kidding. We ain't got time for that." Jeff said, "You said you knew about the affair. Did you ever see Knox or confront him?" I said I didn't. I lied. Pritt was writing something on his paper, stuck up one finger, and said to Savanna, "I'm confused about something. Clear it up for me. Did you stop dating (he threw up air quotes) Knox after you found out about the other women or after you found out he was dealing drugs?" Savanna who was clearly getting agitated stood there with her arms folded and said. "Both revelations came to me about the same time and I ended it. It was just a fling." Whatever that meant. I rolled my eyes at her. Pritt asked us if he could look around. I said, "You've looking around since you been here. If you wanna know If I did it, I didn't. It's obvious that you don't consider Savanna a suspect. You came over here to interview her, but searching her home and interviewing her are two different things. Now, we can't stop you from looking, but we can stop you from searching." He said, "I can go and get a sergeant and a search warrant and come back." I said I knew he could.

It must've been a slow day for them. I'm sure there were more important things they could have been doing. I know I wasn't much of a suspect and they knew it too. They were just doing their jobs. They tried to play hardball with me but I saw right through it. I was a fairly new cop but I knew my rights and I wasn't going to allow them to pressure Savanna into doing or saying anything she felt wasn't right. I knew they weren't going to get a warrant either. They did have to report the interview to their supervisors because I was a police officer. It was all good. He meant it when he said that they weren't going to waste their valuable resources investigating Knox's case. They were going to do the bare minimum. It's a shame that some people warrant quality police service and others don't. After the detectives left Savanna and Edie, who was a close friend to Jasper, talked openly about the incident. It didn't seem to bother Savanna. Maybe it was the Crown Royal she was drinking.

Chapter 12

Turtle was at home playing a video game when a neighbor ran to his house and told him the police and an ambulance was at Jasper's house. He dropped the joystick and ran from his house, past his mother almost knocking her down. When he got to the block, he saw the ambulance's lights on and it made him nervous. As he got closer, he saw Beverly, Jasper's daughter talking to a police officer and both of them were looking into the rear of the ambulance as the attendants worked on Jasper. When Beverly saw Turtle, she ran and embraced him. Turtle asked her what happened and she told him that somebody beat up her dad. Turtle looked at Jasper who appeared to be unconscious. After a few minutes the attendant told the police officer that they were taking him to Trinity hospital. A neighbor who lived two houses down was standing on her porch with her daughter. They approached Turtle, Beverly, and the police officer when the ambulance pulled off. The daughter hugged Beverly and held her hand. Turtle said, "Ms. Anne, can Beverly stay with you? I need to go to the hospital to check on Jasper." Ms. Anne said, "of course she can. C'mon baby." Turtle turned to run home but stopped to go to Jasper's house. He wanted to lock up the house and make sure it was secure. He told the officer who was sitting in his car writing a report, that he wanted to secure Jasper's house and the officer told him that it was okay. Only the outside of the house was a crime scene because Jasper never made it into the house. Turtle looked on the ground near the door and stepped over what looked like blood. When he got in the house he turned to see where the cop was. The officer was still sitting in his cruiser writing a report and Turtle locked the door. Turtle looked where he knew Jasper kept his money and drugs and saw that they were still there. He left them there then checked to see if Jasper's gun was where he kept it. It was. He made sure the back door was locked and that the windows were closed and locked. On his way out he grabbed and ate a piece of chicken and some french fries. "Man, Jasper was a great cook." He also made sure the stove and oven was off. He grabbed Jasper's car keys, turned off the lights and made his way back to the front door. He heard Jasper's cell phone ringing and saw it on the charger. He checked the caller ID and saw that it was Renee. He looked up from the phone, opened the door and was startled to see the officer standing there. "Is everything okay?" Turtle said everything was fine and that he was going to the hospital to see Jasper. He took Jasper's phone with him but didn't answer Renee's call yet. He locked the door behind him and quickly jumped into Jasper's car. He looked at the officer who wasn't paying attention to him and drove to his house to get his driver's license. When he walked into the house his mother asked him what happened. He told her that somebody jumped on Jasper, and he was going to the hospital to check on him. Jasper's phone rang again, and again, it was Renee but he didn't answer it. Not now Renee. Not yet.

When he arrived at Trinity Hospital's emergency entrance, he saw that the ambulance that brought Jasper there was still parked in the emergency fire lane. He went in, gave the receptionist Jasper's name and asked could he see him. A nurse told him to have a seat in the waiting room and she'd call him when he could see him. He went to sit down when Jasper's phone rang. Renee again. He steeled himself, and walked outside to talk to her in private, away from the other people in the waiting room. When he answered the phone, Renee recognized his voice and said, "It must be true. First of all, I know nobody else answers this phone but him, so something must be wrong. Second, I know you got the first three calls and didn't answer that phone. I know you saw that it was me. I'll deal with yo ass later. What happened to Jasper and where's Beverly?" Turtle said, "How did you find out so quickly?" Renee said, "Don't worry about that nigga! Turtle, don't play with me. I got a call that Jasper got beat up." Turtle said, "Renee, please calm down. Beverly is fine. She's down at Ms. Anne's house. I'm at the hospital now. I just got here. I don't know anything else and they won't let me see him yet. I'll call you when I know something. Is that okay?" She said, "Make sure you do and you better not forget!" He said, "Okay. I won't." And he waited for her to hang-up first. Turtle knew exactly who Renee was, what she was capable of, and that she wasn't nobody to mess with. He stood outside to smoke a cigarette before he went back inside.

Turtle sat in the waiting room thinking about Jasper. He looked up to catch a glimpse of CNN on the television mounted on the wall. A homeless man was sleeping in a corner chair with his head against the wall. A lady was there with two boys. One was wearing a Jackie Robinson West little league uniform and had his arm in a sling, and the other one was slumped over sleeping. An older woman was crocheting what looked like a baby's blanket. Turtle went to the vending machine and bought a pop, some cheese crackers and chocolate chip cookies. He looked over and saw the little boy looking at him so Turtle offered him some cookies. The boy looked to his mother for approval, "Mommy?" She said it was okay but she kept a watchful eye on them. He took some cookies and thanked Turtle. He nudged his sleeping brother and offered him some leftovers. Turtle looked at the measly amount the baseball player gave his brother and snickered. He pulled a wad of money from his pocket and treated them to a more snacks. They thanked him as their mother watched them closely. After about an hour Turtle again asked the receptionist how Jasper was. She said he was awake but groggy and that he could see him. She pointed Turtle to the curtained off room where Jasper was. When Jasper saw Turtle, he asked how he was doing. Turtle said, "Me? I should be asking you that question. What the hell happened?" Jasper said, "I really don't know. I walked a female to her car and when I got to my door, somebody came up behind me. I turned around and he hit me. That's all I remember. Where's Beverly?" Turtle said she was fine and down at Ms. Anne's house. Jasper said, "Help me up, I gotta get out of here." Turtle said, "What? You can't leave. Are you okay?" "Yeah, I'm good" he said while wiggling his fingers and toes. The nurse saw Jasper trying to get up and walked over to him. "Baby, what are you doing? You shouldn't leave. We want to check that knot on your head." Jasper gently placed his feet on the ground and stood up. He wanted to try and stand up and walk on his own. He took a few steps and felt like he was good. The nurse handed him something for pain, his discharge instructions and other paperwork. He didn't know who attacked him and felt vulnerable in the hospital. Turtle went to get a wheelchair for Jasper but he said he didn't need it. Jasper went to wait in the waiting room for Turtle to bring the car around. Turtle pulled up right where the ambulance that Jasper came in was once parked and ran to get Jasper. Turtle helped Jasper into the car and waved to the little leaguer and his brother who were kneeled down backwards in their chairs frantically waving back at him.

Jasper laid his head on the headrest, turned to Turtle and said, "You got some cash on you?" Turtle said, "You know I do. What's up?" Jasper said, "I'm wanna go to a hotel for a while and lay low until I figure this thing out." Turtle said, "Renee's been calling like crazy. She told me to keep her updated on your condition. Please call her and let her know I gave you, her message. You know how Renee is. I don't want to get on her bad side again." Jasper closed his eyes while he lay his head on the headrest wondering how he let his guard down. He said, "I'll call her once I'm situated. I can't deal with her right now. She's the last person I want to talk to." Turtle said earnestly, "Okay but remember whenever you talk to her make sure you tell her I gave you the message."

Turtle took Jasper to the Comfort Inn Suites in the suburbs. After he checked him in he went to get Jasper some breakfast at Bob Evans. When Turtle came back Jasper was on the telephone talking to Renee. That was one call he would not be put off. If Jasper didn't call anybody else, he had to call Renee. They didn't talk long because Jasper told Renee that he had to get himself together and that he'd call her back. When he hung up, Turtle said. "Did you tell her I gave you the message?" Jasper said, "Yeah, scared ass nigga I told her." Turtle had good reason to be scared of Renee. He knew her reputation proceeded her and what she had done in the streets when she was younger. Turtle also knew that Renee was Beverly's mother. Beverly knew her mother and she loved her mother. She spent a lot of time with Renee, but lived with Jasper her whole life and knew him as her dominant partner.

Jasper and Turtle talked about what they thought happened. Turtle told him that everything was intact at his house and that nothing appeared to be missing. Jasper thought that maybe it wasn't a robbery attempt after all. Turtle told him about the scary dude who confronted him outside his house on several occasions. Jasper remembered the time someone bearded him in the liquor store parking lot. They compared notes and descriptions; they recalled events, reflected, and rehashed incidents, actions, and scenarios they thought might help them figure out how they let their guards down and who might have done this. Turtle was again frustrated when he couldn't remember specific details. When they described the guy that they each encountered they felt like they were describing the same person to each other. Once Jasper got well he'd sneak by Savanna's house to see if he recognized me as the husband who confronted him in the liquor store parking lot but at that time I still hadn't moved back home yet. It seems like the guy Turtle described outside his house had disappeared because Turtle hadn't seen him again.

After they talked Jasper asked Turtle to go and make a few runs for him. When Turtle left Jasper dreaded calling Renee back but he knew he had to. He knew he had to face that music. He told her he initially thought somebody was about to rob him, but when Beverly came to the door, it scared him off.

But Renee had already heard that Jasper didn't get robbed. She still knew people in the streets. She deduced that it was something else. Jasper asked Renee, "What did Turtle do to you?" He's scared to death of you." She said, "He should be. He knows what he did. You said that you think somebody tried to rob you? It don't sound like a robbery. This might be personal. Are you now messing with somebody's women? Somebody might be sending yo ass a message. I always told you to be careful who you do business with and to not trust everybody. You thought I was trying to tell you what to do but I had your back. Turtle is cool. You can trust him. He ain't smart enough to double cross you. But Edie and Ella, them bitches, I never trusted them especially when you sided with them." He said, "I didn't side"-- She interjected, "Shut up! You did. I know you felt like you had to go into business with them after what happened to their brother, but you said you didn't have anything to do with that. No matter what you tell them they're never going to believe you. They'll never forgive you. They need to let it go but they ain't gonna do it. That happened years ago but I heard that Ella was still talking about it a few weeks ago. I don't know why you're still in the streets. The shop is doing good business and you can make a living doing that. You could have went legit years ago. You were a good cook and could have thrived in the catering business your aunt left you. All those years of learning that business, from your early years in the church. She put everything she had into teaching you that business but you didn't do anything with it. And when was the last time yo ass been to church anyway? I don't know how much longer you gonna be in the streets. I guess as long as you got that trump card to play. Eventually it's gonna run out and won't be able to save you. Maybe this will wake you up, but I doubt it. You're hardheaded and you think your shit don't stink."

"In any event, send me my baby. It won't kill her to stay with me for a little while. I know she's spoiled but she knows when she comes here that I don't play that. A hotel ain't no place for a child to stay. I may not be as good a cook as you are but fast food all the time ain't good either. You're welcome to come too if you want to." When he hung up the telephone, he rolled his eyes and laid his head on the pillow. He knew she was right, as usual, and he didn't dare argue with her.

Chapter 13

Allison, Yvonne, and Jasper were raised in the church. Every Sunday their aunt, their grandmother's sister, took them to church with her and taught them how to cook and cater for large gatherings. She always had them with her, preparing the food in hopes that they'd take over when they got older.

Growing up Jasper never felt pressured to join a gang or sell drugs. The guys in the neighborhood respected the fact that his grandmother sheltered them. When he graduated from high school he either had to get a job, go to college, or join the military. He enrolled in college, worked part-time at Walgreen's and bought him a nice used car.

Although he wasn't in a gang he grew up with the gang members in his neighborhood and smoked reefer and drank wine with them. One day he was with some of the guys and a friend came by when him and another friend was chilling out. The guy said he'd just got into it with some rivals and wanted revenge. The guys were preparing to go and Jasper, not wanting to be seen as a punk, offered to go too. His friend said, "Naw Jasper, this ain't for you. Plus if yo grandmother found out she'd kick yo ass and mines too."

One afternoon when Jasper was at work two sisters came into the store. They just happened to be the younger sisters of a man who sired several children with Jasper's oldest sister. Edie and Ella came in everyday, not to shop but to flirt with him. One day Jasper got up the nerves to ask the more coquettish one, Ella, for her telephone number. They started dating, going to the movies, and hanging out until Ella got bored and moved on. Jasper thought they had something special and was kind of heartbroken when she ended it. He was the Fresh Prince but she wanted Thug Life.

Jasper spent a lot of time at their house. Their older brother Pacman thought he was a well-mannered respectable young man who had potential. Jasper bought weed from him, the best he had smoked up to that time. Pacman enjoyed Jasper's company and asked him if he ever sold weed. Jasper said he hadn't and Pacman told him to give it a try. He gave him ten bags of weed and told him to try to sell them. Jasper left and came back within an hour with Pacman's proceeds. Pacman handed Jasper $30 and ten more bags. Jasper looked at Pacman and said, "Thirty dollars! That's it? That's all I get? I'm the one who took all the risks." Pacman respected his moxie and said he'd consider giving him more if he could do it again. It took him a little bit longer the second time but he did it.

Pacman took Jasper under his wing, taught him the business and they made good money. He still worked at Walgreens but saved all his checks. He didn't waste his money. Pacman taught him to stay lowkey, keep his circle small, and not attract attention to himself. Cell phones were a novelty but he did have one. Pacman taught Jasper to invest in a business and buy himself a home. One thing that Jasper did splurge on was clothes. He liked to dress nicely but not garishly. When Ella saw the change in him, she tried to get back with him but he too had moved on and was expecting a baby with his new girlfriend Renee.

Pacman also had business dealings with some Mexicans who owned a restaurant on the east side of Chicago. The food wasn't great and the restaurant was mostly a front for selling drugs and guns. How the hell can you have a Mexican restaurant and not make a good taco? Whenever Pacman needed to send the Mexicans something Jasper took it to them. What Jasper did was similar to what Turtle would do for him years later. Pacman told Jasper to make sure he always had his driver's license. He knew Jasper didn't look like he was in the streets like other drug dealers and felt the police were less likely to stop him. Another important thing was that Jasper didn't smoke or drink on the days he dropped off. After the deal was over he could smoke or drink all he wanted. Edie was more serious and interested in the business aspect. Sometimes she'd ride with Jasper when he went to the Mexican's restaurant.

Chapter 14

One afternoon Jasper was at Pacman's house and they were barbequing, drinking, and smoking. The Mexicans called and asked Pacman if they could get some weed. This would be outside of the normal way they did business. They had a set schedule when Jasper went to the restaurant. This was against everything Pacman believed in. He never made impulsive decisions when it came to transactions especially if it involved him driving under the influence of alcohol or drugs. But he knew they didn't want just a few bags. If they called, they wanted at least a pound of marijuana. He knew the Mexicans well, they had been doing business for a while. He decided to confer with his partners Edie and Jasper. Edie said if they wanted it bad enough, they should come to them. Pacman didn't want them to know where he lived so that was out of the question. Jasper suggested that they meet at a neutral location but they claimed to not be familiar with the south side. After they mulled it over for a while Jasper said he'd go to the restaurant but only if they made it worth his while. Pacman said they agreed to send something him and Jasper could profit from. Jasper said he'd do it, plus he wanted to buy more liquor.

Pacman went into his garage and got a pound of weed. He put it in a leather bag and gave it to Jasper. Pacman also sent them something else and told Jasper to see if they wanted that too. Jasper said he wanted to drive Pacman's newest car and listen to Pacman's new Eric B and Rakim cassette. When Jasper was leaving, he noticed that Ella was right behind him. She claimed to want to get some things to make daiquiris with. Jasper didn't have the energy to argue with her. He just wanted to go and handle that business, and get back to enjoying the rest of his day.

Jasper knew Ella was up to something and figured it out when he noticed that she changed from wearing blue jeans to now wearing a short skirt. He had to admit that she did look good and he tried to ignore her. However, that Bacardi Black he was drinking made things hard, literally speaking. He thought a little rap music might take his mind off his passenger but she was relentless. He put the cassette in and "To The Listeners" came on. She waited until he pulled off and tried to change the cassette. They slapped each other's hands and she pressed the eject button, snatched the cassette out, and threw it on the backseat. He looked at her and nodded his head. They were fussing and cussing at each other all while he tried to reach the cassette. He turned for a second to place his hand on the cassette but when he looked up, he was too close to the car in front of him and slammed into it.

Jasper must've hit his head on the steering wheel and blacked out. He bit this lip and tasted blood. He looked in the passenger's seat and saw that Ella was gone. A police officer opened his door and asked him if he were alright. He nodded that he was but when he tried to step out the car, he fell to the ground. An ambulance was called but after they checked his vitals, he refused further service. However, the police officer smelled alcohol on his breath and determined that he had been drinking. The officer handcuffed him and walked him to his car. When he sat down, he looked out the window and saw people looking at him in the car. He also saw Ella standing on the sidewalk with the other pedestrians. The police officer retrieved the leather bag from his car and put it on the floor of the front seat of their car. They took him to the 4th district police station where he'd probably be arrested for DUI and possession of a controlled substance.

The uniformed officer took Jasper to an interrogation room, uncuffed one hand, and cuffed it to a ring that was mounted on the wall. He told Jasper to removed everything from his pockets and put the contents in a clear plastic bag that he handed him. The officer stood a few feet away from Jasper watching him slowly empty his pockets and place everything on the table that was in front of him. Jasper thought about his life, what he knew was in the bag, and his baby and he started to cry. The officer said, "Don't cry now, little brotha. You should have thought about that before you started selling drugs. You really don't look like you are from the streets. You look like a church boy. I'm gonna do you a favor. I called somebody who might help you. But you gotta be truthful with him. He can smell bullshit from a mile away." Jasper wiped his nose with his shirt.

A few minutes later a police officer wearing a ponytail, faded blue jeans, cowboy boots, and a T-Shirt that said 'Humpty Dumpty Was Pushed' came into the room. The uniformed police officer showed him the contents of the bag and both of them looked at Jasper. He went and sat on the table where Jasper's things were and asked him where he got the weed from. "Are you picking it up or dropping it off? I see that you only have $175.00 so you were on your way to sell it. Right? We ran your name for wants and warrants and you are clear. You've never been arrested before. Never. You've never even had a traffic ticket. Either you're really good at avoiding arrests or we're really bad at identifying you. It's rare in this business that I come across a young black man who's first contact with the police is delivery of a pound of cannabis. That's crazy! You do have a valid driver's license and your Toyota Corolla has all its tags. What the hell man! But the car you were driving is a different story. Who is Edie Holcomb?" Jasper said a friend. The cop continued, "Whoever let you drive in that condition doesn't care about you. They wouldn't have driven drunk with a pound of weed. Let me tell you something, you ain't ready for this. Give it up before you get in too deep. This life ain't for you." Jasper listened to every word he said. The officer moved in closer to Jasper even though there wasn't anyone else in the room. "Listen to me, I can make this whole thing go away, the DUI, the weed. I can't do anything about the accident but I'll tell you this, the other driver didn't have a license either and I'm sure you and him can settle this out of court and not involve your insurance companies. I'm sure you and Ms. Holcomb have some expendable cash laying around. I can look at you and tell this ain't your weed. I know you're working for someone else. If you work with me, if you give me some information I can use, I'll work with you. You don't have to be arrested today. You wouldn't make it in the County let alone prison. If you keep this up that's exactly where you're going, either there or the cemetery. I've been doing this for years. You won't make it son. Give it up. Mull it over for a while. I'll be back."

Jasper had never been in trouble before. He never wanted to disappoint his mother. He could not deal with the ignominy of being arrested for selling drugs. He didn't know exactly what this officer wanted but he knew he wanted this nightmare to be over, and fast.

After a few minutes both officers came back into the room with the leather bag and the Humpty Dumpty sympathizer now had on rubber gloves. He pulled a chair close to Jasper and sat down. He took the marijuana from the leather bag and said, "We weighed the marijuana and it came up to a almost a pound. How much would you have gotten from the sale of this?" Not really expecting an answer. He continued, "When I send this marijuana to the crime lab, they are going to lift your fingerprints from the plastic. You didn't know we lifted fingerprints from plastic did you? I'll include this in my report;

"Police officers responded to a call of a traffic accident and discovered subject passed out behind the wheel. A Chicago Fire Department ambulance was called to assist the driver who subsequently refused service. The responding officers attempted to conduct a field sobriety test because he reeked of alcohol but he was unable to perform thereby failing it. He was taken into custody and during a subsequent search of the vehicle a leather bag containing a green leafy plant-like substance suspect cannabis was recovered. Subject was the lone occupant in the vehicle and he did not have a driver's license in his possession. A subsequent report from the crime lab revealed that subject's prints, yours, were lifted from the cannabis. It will be a delivery of cannabis case, in oppose to a possession case because contrary to how you or your lawyer might try and spin it, no judge or jury is going to believe that you were going to smoke a pound of marijuana. That's what will be in my report. Case closed."

They both looked at Jasper, then walked away to let that sink in. Jasper leaned his head against the wall, closed his eyes and sighed. The police officers came back a few minutes later and talked amongst themselves. Jasper, in a cracked voice, said, "Officer, what will I have to do?" He said, "I want to know where you got the weed and where you were going with it. I want you to work with me and my team. I need to trust you and I need for you to trust me. But if I find out you are lying to me, any deal we have is off and I am sending you away."

Jasper was not about to tell on Pacman. He told the cops he worked for a guy named Trey. He told them about the Mexicans and that they couldn't make a good burrito. They couldn't believe it. He thought the officers were satisfied with the information he gave them.

The officer said, "I'm a man of my word. You gave us some valuable information that we might be able to use. But if I find out you held back, our deal is over. I'm not going to charge you with the weed or with the DUI. But you gotta trust me with this. I can't let you just walk out that door." Jasper teared up again. This guy you work for, Trey, he knows by now that you've been arrested. He knows what he gave you and it's gonna look suspicious if you showed up tomorrow. He probably knows that this is your first arrest and that you'll probably make bail. So we're gonna sit you down for a while. I talked to my watch commander and he agreed to cooperate. We're charging you with several traffic violations and we're gonna drag your paperwork. So go on back to lock-up and use the time to figure out what you want to do with the rest of your life."

But keep in mind that this weed ain't going no where. If you agree to work with us evidently, it's gonna go away. Otherwise," while keeping his gaze on Jasper, and pointing to the marijuana with his pen, He said, "What do you think I'm gonna do with that?" I think there's more to this whole restaurant, Mexican's thing. Having someone like you who's on the inside is big. I think we can do big things. There may even be an opportunity for you to make a little something on the side." Jasper said, "What if I get caught?" The officer said, "How? All you're doing is notifying us what you're taking there and if you're picking something up. You're not meeting us anywhere. It's only a phone call. It's that simple." Jasper thought it over and tentatively agreed to do it. The officer said, "My name is Waylon James, yeah like the singer Waylon Jennings. My father was a huge fan. You can call me Lonnie. I'm going to give you a telephone number to memorize and you can call me anytime, 24/7." Jasper nodded yes again.

When it was time for Lonnie to take Jasper to lock-up, he said, "Are you ready?" Jasper nodded his head and grabbed his things. Jasper was about to go through the most humiliating times of his life. Since he had never been locked up he didn't know what to expect. When he got in lock-up there was already a guy there waiting to be processed. He got there just as the guys were eating their lunch. They had a slab of ribs, rib tips and french fries with barbeque sauce on them all from Leon's BBQ. He was still hungover, had the munchies and knew that Pacman had a feast at his house. The police officer who worked lock-up told him that he would have to go through a thorough search because last week a guy who was being locked up for the first time smuggled a razor in his shoe and tried to commit suicide. And they were taking extra precautions. He told Jasper and the other guy to take off their clothes and shoes. They couldn't have their belts or his shoestrings. He told them to open their mouths using their pinky fingers. He made him squat down and open their cheeks, then turn around and lift up their sacks. The officer was distracted and taking his sweet time. He had Jasper and the other guy standing there butt naked while he slowly and meticulously went through each piece of their clothing. The officers were watching a baseball game and offering color commentaries like they were experts.

It had been a few days since Jasper got locked-up. He wondered what did Lonnie mean when he said he'd be locked-up for a little while. Every time someone did their rounds he asked them was it his time to get out but he never go an answer. When he did finally doze off it wasn't a good sound sleep. Every little sound woke him up. The guy in the cell next to him kept kicking the cell door all night. His cell smelled like old stale clothes, sweat, and urine. He didn't have a blanket or a pillow and it was so cold that he took his arms out of his sleeves and held them close to his body to keep warm. The drinking water was warm and the sandwiches were cold. There was a puddle of something on his floor. Every time someone made bond he wondered when was his turn coming. All kinds of crazy things entered his mind. Did Lonnie figure out that he lied about Pacman? Did he renege on their agreement and decide to send him to the County after all?

When Ella made it home, she told Pacman about the accident and that the police had the weed. He called Allison and wanted to devise a plan to tell their mother and Jasper's job. They told his mother that Jasper was offered a management position at Walgreens and would need to go to a three-day retreat to learn the new job. His mother asked why he hadn't told her. Allison told her mother, "Mama, I was standing right there when he told us." They told Walgreens that he had a family emergency and left town suddenly. However, nobody had a plan for Renee who had been calling the house like crazy.

Ella took Allison and the kids home after they spent a day with Pacman. When they pulled up to the house, they saw Renee's car parked out front. They quickly grabbed the kids and ran into the house. The baby was playing with the grandmother and Renee was looking through a photo album. "Hey mama Knox, I got a picture of Beverly and it looks exactly like this picture you have of Jasper." When Renee looked up and saw Ella she got an immediate attitude. There was no love lost between them two and it was obvious to everyone except Allison's mom. The kids started playing with the baby, Renee pointed to Allison and said, "Can I have a word with you?" Renee led Allison to a corner of the basement and said, "What the hell is going on?! What's up with this Walgreens manager story? Where is Jasper?" They heard footsteps coming down the stairs, turned and saw Ella. Renee said, "Excuse me. Can I help you?" Ella put her hands on her hips, and Renee said, "Not now bitch! This is not the time." Allison stepped in between them and told Ella to go back upstairs. Allison told Renee about the accident, the arrest, and the lies they told Jasper's mother and Walgreens. Renee was pissed but she understood why they lied. Allison asked Renee if Beverly could stay the night with them and play with the kids. Renee said it was okay and she wanted to get out of there before she got into it with Ella. She didn't want Jasper's mother to see that side of her.

Jasper was finally released after more than two days. He felt like that was longer than a little while. When they let him out he had the plastic bag that contained his property. In the other hand he had a sandwich that they offered him. His embarrassment quickly turned to relief. He called Pacman and told him to pick him up but said he was going to start walking home. He wanted to get as far away from there as quickly as he could.

Pacman pulled up right behind Jasper and blew the horn. Jasper turned to look at a car that he had never seen before. He ran around to the passenger's seat and embraced Pacman and gave him some dap. Pacman rolled down his window and said, "Damn, nigga you stank!"

They went to Pacman's house where Allison was waiting for him. She grabbed and hugged her little brother but abruptly released him because of his stench. He jumped in the shower and put on some of Pacman's clothes. They updated him on the lies they told to his mother and his job. Allison told him to make sure to call Renee's crazy ass as soon as possible. Nobody needed to tell him to do that. After things settled down, he told Pacman what he had went through, everything minus his plans with Lonnie. He knew he had to go and face his mother, and more importantly, Renee.

After a few days, Jasper was back at work and stocking some shelves when someone came up behind him and called his name. He turned around to see Lonnie standing there. Lonnie had a piece of paper in his hand and said, "Hey buddy. How are you doing? Remember me? Don't forget our deal. Here's my number." And he handed Jasper a piece of paper. Jasper took the number and shoved it into his pocket.

Chapter 15

When I was finally reinstated back to full duty after what was in my opinion a bogus investigation for using excessive force, June updated me on what had been going on. I met a lot of good people while at the callback unit. They were going through some tough times in their lives. The police officer who smoked marijuana was relieved of duty as a police officer and fired. The police officer who shot and killed the young man was exonerated and reassigned. When the civilian investigator asked him why he didn't shoot the subject in the leg to stop him, he said, "We're not trained to shoot in the leg. We're trained to shoot to kill. Head shots and body shots are what's on my target boards." He was subsequently assigned to be an instructor at the police academy. My accuser should have known that our investigators we're going to dig into his personal life and uncover those domestic battery accusations his wife filed on him. Light-skinned niggas ain't that bright.

June told me that him and some his friends from the academy went out drinking one night. I said, "You ain't go no male friends so who are these friends? Females? Does Dorena know about these friends you hang out with?" He said, "They are just friends, no she doesn't know about them, and--

anyway, let me finish my story. I put in a transfer to go and work in the 17th district. It's closer to home and I'm tired of this long commute. I'll go from a 40-minute drive to a 10-minute drive." I told him that he only wanted to transfer so that he could be closer to Dorena. He didn't deny it. He continued, "We're still young and early in our careers. At this rate, if we stay in this busy district, we're gonna burn ourselves out before we're thirty years old. Being a cop on the south side and west side Chicago de-sensitizes you. We see and experience so much that it makes you cold and callous. We gotta learn to be judicious." I said, "Judicious?" He said, "Yeah, judicious. You do know what judicious means don't you? Didn't they teach you that in those schools you always brag about going to? We gotta be smart when it comes to the choices we make. We drink and smoke and eat fast food everyday. If you could you'd eat a half of chicken from Harold's once a week. Fried chicken is good but you people over do it. Do you know what people in the 17th district consider serious crimes? Taggers. People who write graffiti on walls and garages. That's a serious offense to them. You should think about transferring too. I talked to Whitey and he said he's sick of working in the 9th district." I said, "The commute will be good for you but I'd go from a 5-minute drive to a 45-minute drive." June said, You and Savanna can move out there, y'all can get a fresh start in a new neighborhood. I'm sure they got Black people out there. And that way you can keep closer tabs on her." It sounded good and I didn't deny that it was a good idea.

"The other big thing that's been going on is that the white boys have been recovering a record number of guns from the streets. "Is it derogatory when I refer to them as white boys? I wonder how they feel about that. I've never heard them call us black boys or brown boys. I'm sure they've called us worse."

Chapter 16

Police officers approached their duties in different ways. Police work is not a monolith. Some officers were community oriented. They enjoyed going into the community they served and getting to know the citizens and business owners. They actually got out of their cars and walked the beat. They dedicated their time to community policing.

Officer Reynolds was the imposing police officer I met early in my career. I thought they called him Rap as a play on words because of his name but they called him Rap because he was always rapping about something. "When people call the police, first they see blue, then they see black. You have a moral obligation to do something substantive when you serve our people and our community. When those other officers serve their communities, you can bet that their people get the best service. And our people deserve it too. People should have wanted to give you the thumbs up after you've left their house in opposed to the middle finger." He was a member of the Afro-American Police League and argued that they should have a more prominent role when it came to negotiating issues that were important to us. Our Union claimed to represent all police officers equally but nevertheless, the AAPL should have at least had a seat at the table.

The more aggressive police officers liked the chase of getting drugs and guns off the streets. They focused more on getting bad guys, killers, robbers, and burglars. That's also where the real money lie, in going to court and doing overtime. The white boys we worked with liked identifying and finding stolen cars. That's what got them pumped.

The veteran officers taught them how to identify stolen cars, how to write reports, and how to get charges approved at the State's Attorney's office. There is a difference between stealing a car and being in possession of a stolen vehicle. The lines were blurred but they used that knowledge for themselves and to their advantage when they had suspects. They learned to separate the occupants when they caught them in stolen cars and get information from them. That information, and those arrests, usually led to other charges for drugs, and the thing they loved most, recovering guns. The bosses loved recovered firearms.

Chapter 17

I ran into Malik, Curly, and Baby J. quite often. The first time was in the parking lot of ("CVS") High School.

June took off early one day and I rode around by myself. Ordinarily I would have taken off too but I decided to stay at work. I went to Jewel-Osco grocery store to grab a few things and the fried chicken they were frying smelled so good that I bought eight pieces. When I came out, I saw an elderly couple standing by their car, which was parked next to mines, and they were looking at their flat tire. I couldn't just get into my car and drive away. I asked the man if he had a spare and he said he had a donut in his trunk. I was the least mechanical person I knew but I could change a tire. The lady was standing outside shivering so I started my car and told her she could sit inside while we changed the tire. "Y'all hurry up, I don't want my sherbet to melt." I was proud of myself for changing the tire so quickly. I told them I'd follow them home since they didn't live too far away. When we got to the house they parked right in front of their house. I helped them take their grocery bags to the door and the woman tried to hand me a $10 bill. I told her I couldn't take it. She said, " I'm pretty sure that's no part of your job." She was adamant about me taking it but I was just as adamant about not taking it. I said, "There is something you can do for me. Can I please wash my hands?" She said, "Absolutely." As we approached the steps, I heard somebody down the block yelling, "Granddaddy, grandma, you alright?!" I turned to see several guys running towards us. It was Malik, Curly, and Baby J. Malik looked at me with disdain as I smiled and walked past him into his grandparent's house.

When I got inside, I handed her the bag and she looked for her sherbet. She took the sherbet out and hurried it to the freezer. The grandfather pointed me towards the bathroom. I washed my hands using a fresh smelling soap from a dispenser and shook my hands dry. When I came out, she handed me a couple of paper towels. She walked into the kitchen and her husband explained to the guys what happened and why I was in their house. I asked him was he good. He said, "I'm gonna call my brother and have him carry me to Sears to get a tire. Can I offer you something, a cup of coffee or a pop?" I said no thank you. His wife came from the kitchen and said, "That chicken sure did smell good. What are you gonna eat with it?" I said, "I don't know, probably some French fries." She said, "No vegetables?" I said, "Can I ask you a question? How would you feel if you came home from work, or from church, and some guys were sitting in a car in front of your house drinking liquor and throwing their trash on the ground?" She said, "I'd have a fit! I would march right out there and tell them that they had to leave. Anybody on this block would do that. Why?" I looked at Malik, smirked, and nodded my head. His grandparents also looked at him. The grandfather said, "If you're ever in the neighborhood feel free to stop by anytime." I told him I would. Grandma continued, "And if you see any of these." pointing at the three of them, "in any mischief, you have my permission to knock them upside their heads and bring them here. I raised their mamas and I raised them." Malik rolled his eyes at me but he didn't dare disrespect his grandparents.

CHAPTER 18

June and I went to the station so he could use the bathroom and I could use the telephone. My sergeant walked over to me holding a piece of paper and I quickly ended my call. He said, "A lady called the Commander's office and said that when she came home from work, she found drugs in her mailbox. I need you guys to go over there and check it out for me. Now listen, this lady is a close friend of the Commander's and she was his Sunday school teacher so give this the due diligence it deserves." He flashed a portentous smile at me, handed me the piece of paper that had her name and address on it, and walked away. I thought to myself, maybe he thought highly of us to assign a job that was so important. When June came out of the bathroom, I told him about our job but doubted that he shared my sentiment.

On the way to the lady's house, I told June, "Lately you've been hostile and argumentative when it comes to dealing with my people. I know you are going through some things but you can't take it out on them." He said, "I don't know what you're talking about. I'm good." I said, "remember the man who wanted a report because his window was broken out? You said his house stank and his wife was fat. When we walked into his house you said, 'Whew, sir do me a favor, put your cats away I'm allergic to them.' He said he didn't have any cats and you blurted out, "Then why does it smell like salmon croquettes and kitty litter in here?' When you asked him about the dress that was hanging up, he said it was an anniversary gift he was giving to his wife. You looked at the picture of the two of them and said you didn't think she'd be able to fit it. He didn't ask you that June. I'm sure he knew his wife's dress size." June said, "I was honest with him. I told him the truth. That dress would not have fit the woman in that picture. If he wasn't sure of her size he should have given her a blender or a gift card or something like that. What if she tried the dress on and it was too small?" I nodded my head and said, "June, this lady who's house we're going to knows the Commander personally. She could have called the non-emergency number and had anybody come to her house but she called directly to his office. The sergeant said she was the Commander's Sunday school teacher. I know church people. I can relate to church folk." June said, "Is it because you're black? And when was the last time you been to church anyway?" I said, "It's been a while, but that's not the point. Let me do the talking." I held up the piece of paper and said, "I got this. Ida Mae Dunbar is about to get the best police service, ever!" June threw up his hands and said, "Okay. Fine."

We came across two officers who were conducting a street stop. They had several guys on their car, guys we knew pretty well. We couldn't just drive by them without stopping and assisting them. Officer Keane was the leader of a cabal of police officers who had been making a lot of arrests by recovering illegal guns from the streets. He was searching a guy all the way to the right while his partner, Peggy Delgado, stood to the far left watching the other guys. I gave Keane a head nod, and walked next to Delgado and asked her if she minded if I search one of her subjects. It was a courtesy. I couldn't just walk up and start searching the guy. She said it was okay and seemed appreciative that we were there to assist them. One of the guys who I knew always had weed on him looked away from me when I walked right up flush on him and whispered, "Where's it at?" He didn't say anything so I repeated myself, "Malik, where's it at?" He turned to me, close enough to kiss me and said, "It's in my draws."

When I saw Delgado, it reminded me of what these same guys said about her a few weeks earlier; "I thought women officers were suppose to call a male officer if she had a male suspect to search. I heard male officers call for a female officer if he had a female suspect to search." I said, "Any officer can search any suspect if they feel that there is an imminent threat like if a person might have a weapon. We don't have to wait for a same sex officer to assist us." He said, "She never waits. If she's working with another female she's going to search us. And I must admit, we don't really mind. Sometimes she violates us. She's disrespectful. If she thinks niggas got something down in their draws, she's going down there to get it! She moves things around, if you know what I mean."

I was familiar with all these guys and I know they watched me closely. While I was patting Malik down, I felt his cigarettes, his lighter, and his pack of Now & Later candy. "Let me get one" I said and ate one without waiting for him to say yes or no. I told him to raise his leg and felt that he had some money in his sock. I took it out and handed it to him. I patted his stomach and moved down to where his weed was. I patted it to let him know that I knew it was there. I announced he was clean and moved on to the next guy. He looked at me and seemed relieved. I searched the next guy but he didn't have anything on him. All the guys probably knew Malik had weed but now they knew that I knew it too. They probably would have preferred that Delgado search them and maybe move some things around for them. Not today guys. Maybe next time.

While we were assisting them some of Keane's acolytes showed up. Keane was the kind of guy who liked to talk shit. Him and Malik went back and forth at each other, they were signifying and playing the dozens. Malik was from the streets and on his home turf and got the best of Keane. Keane couldn't match his wit, timing, and delivery. Malik had the confidence of a stand-up comedian. Keane was on the verge of making it personal while Malik kept it professional. June felt like had we not been there Keane probably would have called him a nigger or tried to provoke him to do something that Keane could arrest him for.

When Keane released the guys from the street stop, he went and sat in the car because he didn't want to hear us teasing him. He smirked and said magnanimously, "Ha, ha, ha, very funny. Go ahead and get it out of your system." He knew that he let Malik get the best of him. Keane probably thought Malik was intimidated by his blue uniform or his white skin. He wasn't. Malik stood up to the bully even though he was the one who was in a submissive position of being a black man with his hands on a police car during a street stop. He never disrespected Keane and let him know that he wasn't going to be disrespected either. Keane will think twice about doing that again. And we didn't let up either. We stood outside smoking cigarettes, teasing, and ribbing Keane who had turned beet red. Then I remembered our job, "Oh shit! C'mon June, let's go!"

When we were back in route to Ida Mae Dunbar's house, I reminded June that I was in charge and for him to take a supporting role. He looked out of the window aimlessly and I didn't appreciate that he didn't acknowledge or respect my authority.

When we pulled up to the house, we saw someone looking out of the curtains. I said, "June" and patted my chest with my hand telling him that I had this. A lady pushed open her wrought iron screen door as we walked up the stairs. She looked us up and down as we walked past her and into her home. Ida Mae Dunbar was wearing a housecoat over her blouse and skirt. She had huge hands, big feet, and was wearing a tiny leather wrist watch that was fastened in the last hole. She was old enough to be our grandmother. Mrs. Dunbar lived in a beautiful raised ranch style house. There was plastic covering on her sectional sofa pieces. I was drawn to these beautiful laminated posters on the walls with Bible Scriptures, verses, and quotes;

"Surely the LORD is in this place and I wasn't even aware of it."- Genesis 28:16, and "As for me and my family, we will serve the LORD."- Joshua 24:15.

Throughout the house were sepia pictures of people posed in caps & gowns and military uniforms. Portraits of The Lord JESUS Christ and The Last Supper, and official photos of President John F. Kennedy, Rev. Dr. Martin Luther King Jr. and Mayor Harold Washington were also on the walls. The floor was carpeted but worn down and had runners and throw rugs on them. A piano was in the adjoining living room. She had an older dining room set with eight chairs and the matching cabinet. Table mats were set, and in the center of the table was a bowl that contained fake fruit, miscellaneous pieces of mail, utility bills, and a Guidepost magazine. Surely I shared a kindred spirit with this woman.

I got in professional police mode, ready to give my Commander's Sunday school teacher my very best service. "Good evening ma'am, how are you doing this evening and how can we help you?" She wasn't buying it and came out of a bag on us. "Where the devil y'all been?! I called Booman's office over an hour ago." June and I looked at each other and mouthed out "Booman" She continued, "When I got home from work I went to check the mailbox and found drugs in my box." I asked her where they were and she said, "Where you think they are? They still in the mailbox! And I smell cigarette smoke. Are y'all supposed to be smoking?" I walked past her and June and went to the mailbox. I shone my flashlight into the mailbox then reached inside and pulled out a plastic bag that did have what looked like drugs. I walked back to where they were standing and showed it to them. She said, "What is that and who put it in my mailbox?" I said, "Lady, how the hell you expect us to know. It was in your mailbox." Almost immediately I remembered those pictures and posters on the wall. Then the next thing I know, whop! a backhand to my mouth. I never saw it coming. She said, "Watch your mouth in here young man. Watch your tone with me." I bowed my head in submission, my eyes watered, I bit my swollen bottom lip and said, "Yes, ma'am." June didn't know what to say so he told her we were going to take the drugs back to the station and conduct a full investigation, whatever that meant. He tried to explain the process of writing a report to her in a way she'd understand but she never broke her gaze from me. I kept my eyes on her hands not wanting to get hit with another one. June kept talking way too much, babbling on and on about nothing. Finally he said, "You'd better be careful you don't trip on one of those throw rugs, fall and hit your head on that piano." I apologized profusely again and tried to avoid eye contact with Mrs. Dunbar. I ducked out as quickly as possible with my tail between my legs. I couldn't get out of there fast enough. When we got back in the car June said, "You handled that one well, church boy."

When we got back to the station, I found our sergeant. He looked at my lip and said, "Whatever you said, I bet you won't say that again. Didn't you ever go to Sunday school?" I didn't say anything, I just showed him what we had. He asked me what it was. I said I thought it was cocaine. He thought it was heroin. June and I were so green that we didn't know exactly what it was. It wasn't like in the movies when you test it by putting some on your tongue. He asked one of the tactical officers to help us write the report and inventory it.

When we finished the paperwork, I went to look for my sergeant again.

When I found him I said, "Am I in trouble with the Commander?"

He said, "In trouble for what?"

"For what happened at Mrs. Dunbar's house."

"What happened at Mrs. Dunbar's house?"

"You don't know? The Commander doesn't know? I said something... and"

"And what?"

I said, "Why did you say what you said to me when we came back?"

He flashed that smile again and said, "What happened to you, happened to the Commander when he was a young officer. It happened to me too. Ida Mae don't play. She's been around for a long time and she takes matters into her own hands. Mrs. Dunbar never told us anything. She never has and she probably never will."

I said, "Can she get away with that?"

He said, "Would you like to file a formal complaint against the Commander's Sunday school teacher and have her arrested?" I rubbed my swollen lips together and nodded no. He said, "You never saw it coming did you?" I shook my head and walked away.

Chapter 19

Maeve loved family outings especially when everybody was together. She loaded Robbie, the kids, and the neighbors' kid into the minivan once a month and they spent the entire day first at the shopping mall, then at Sam's Club, and finally at either Shakey's, Ryan's, or Old Country Buffett. She loved the spaciousness of Sam's Club. The kids sampled everything the store offered and she always bought way more than what she needed. "Could my family possibly go through ninety-six rolls of toilet paper in a month?"

She loved the bakery section and always bought a spiral sliced honey baked ham. The kids were allowed to get a bag or box of their favorite cereal or candy and Robbie always got a case or two of his favorite beer. When they approached the beer section Robbie didn't seem all that excited about getting his favorite beer. He had been distracted for the last couple of days. He snapped out of his trance briefly when his daughter tried to pick up a case of her dad's favorite beer. Maeve said, "Robbie, are you okay?" He said, "Yeah, I'm good." She noticed that he hadn't been himself lately. She knew that cops dealt with a lot of issues and had a lot on their minds.

Whenever he had problems at work, he never brought them home in the past. He said it was nothing.

But it wasn't nothing. It was something to him. Maeve knew that it wasn't another woman who had his attention. What she didn't know was that it was another man.

It had been several days since Robbie Keane got into a war of words with Malik. When he should have been enjoying his family on his days off, all he thought about was Malik getting the best of him, and he couldn't let it go. It had been 3 days! He felt like Malik embarrassed and humiliated him in front of his peers. And he did. But Keane started it. Now he wanted revenge. He wanted blood. Every dude that resembled Malik bought back memories of that day. He couldn't wait to get back to work. He couldn't wait to see Malik again. But why? What was he going to do to Malik? If he didn't find him, was the next young black man at his mercy if he mouthed off to him? He thought to himself, "I'm not going to let another young black dude get the best of me. After all, I'm the police." Some police officers are wired that way. They let their pride get in the way.

Chapter 20

Jasper had been working with Lonnie and his team for several weeks. He called Lonnie once a week to tell him that he was dropping something off to the Mexicans or picking something up for Trey. He wasn't always truthful with Lonnie about what he dropped off or picked up. There were times when Jasper did runs for Pacman but he never told Lonnie anything.

Every so often Lonnie would surprise Jasper and pop up at the Walgreens. One day Lonnie showed up and he was holding a box of Just for Mens in his hand. "Who's Pacman? And do not lie to me. In case you haven't figured it out yet, every now and then we'll tail you. You're not the only person we got working for us. Some intel we gathered points to a big-time player named Pacman who does a lot of business with the Mexicans. That intel also told us that you and him are partners. I need to know who he is and why you never told us about him." Jasper looked Lonnie directly in his eyes, then looked past him to see Ella walking towards them. Jasper said, "Sir, that product you want is right over here." He said hello to Ella, and escorted him to another aisle. When they got far enough away from Ella, Jasper said, "That's his sister. I'll call you as soon as I can. I promise. Now please leave." Lonnie nodded that he was leaving but said, "I'll be expecting that call today" and he left. Jasper went to find Ella and said, "What's up?" She said, "Nothing. Who was that?" He said, "Just a customer who had the wrong brand of hair dye." Ella knew it didn't look right but she didn't say anything else. She went to get what she came for and left. Lonnie sat outside in his personal car and waited for Ella to come out. When she came out and got into her car, he wrote down the make, model, and license plates to the car she was driving.

When Jasper finally called Lonnie, he didn't tell him everything about Pacman. Lonnie knew that he could no longer trust all the information that Jasper gave him, and he knew what he had to do. He didn't rely on the information that Jasper provided. It was time for him and his team to act. They had gotten more than enough information about Pacman or Trey and the Mexicans from their other snitches.

Jasper still hadn't told Pacman about Lonnie. Whenever Jasper left his house for any reason, he thought that Lonnie or his team might be watching or following him. He'd take different cars as if that was gonna throw Lonnie and his team off track. Whenever he went to the restaurant, he might take a different route.

Whenever Jasper went to the restaurant, he always parked in the same parking lot across the street. He got out, nervously looked around and retrieved the bag from the trunk. As he was entering the restaurant, an officer walked in with him and announced that they were conducting a search warrant. Lonnie and about a dozen police officers were right behind them. Lonnie grabbed Jasper by the arm and took the bag from his hand. Several officers went behind the counter and into the kitchen and brought two cooks out to the front.

The waitress was also seated and all three were searched and handcuffed. And of course she was the only one who spoke English. A family was eating but they were interviewed and released. They ate free that day. Lonnie's team thoroughly searched the whole restaurant but found nothing but mice droppings and other health-related violations. Lonnie tried to make small talk with Jasper but he wouldn't talk back. He also tried talking to the Mexicans but they also refused to talk. Lonnie finally placed the bag on the table, opened it and reached inside. The only things that were in the bag were three brand new pairs of newly re-released Air Jordan Air Force Ones and a couple of Maze featuring Frankie Beverly cassettes. When it came to Air Jordan's and the music of Frankie Beverly and Maze, they were fan favorites in our community. We had to have the old school stuff.

A couple of weeks after the search warrant Pacman disappeared. Allison knew something but she wasn't talking. Ella found out about the search warrant at the restaurant and knew Jasper didn't get arrested. She felt like Jasper knew a lot more than he admitted. He tried to explain to Edie and Ella that there was nothing in the bag but knew they didn't believe him. Ella knew how Pacman operated and that he dealt with the Mexicans for years. She thought that whatever Jasper took to the Mexicans was recovered by the police and he cooperated to save his own ass. Ella was openly critical towards Jasper and didn't trust him. Edie told her to try and hold it together until they found out what happened to their brother. In the meantime, they would try and run Pacman's businesses and collect the rent from his tenants. Edie knew that they couldn't do it by themselves and that Jasper could help them. Allison had the keys to the shop, to the buildings, and Pacman's money. Edie knew she had to make nice with

Allison and Jasper, but Ella resisted. Jasper wanted to keep the peace and make sure his sister, and her kids, got treated fairly. There was an underlying friction between the families but they got through it. They did everything together and openly. They paid the mortgage on Pacman's shop, buildings, and his house, and paid his other bills, the ones they knew of. And they made sure Allison and the kids were taken care of. Allison eventually conceded responsibility to Jasper and he took over for her. Him and Edie continued working together and maintained a cordial relationship. Edie and Ella still worked at the shop, managed it, and ran it as smoothly as they could.

Chapter 21

Word on the streets was that the Mexicans who owned the restaurant were looking for Jasper. They thought he set them up because the city shut them down due to their many health code violations. It was probably that and the fact that their food sucked.

The Mexicans knew that most Black people frequented Evergreen Plaza so they often went there looking for Jasper. Years later June told me that they called it Everblack Plaza. One day Jasper and Renee were there and the Mexicans recognized and approached them. They were the same Mexicans from the restaurant but now, miraculously, they spoke fluent English. When they got close enough to Jasper, one of the guys opened his coat so Jasper could see the gun that was in his waistband. He told Jasper to walk with them to the parking lot, while the other guy grabbed Renee by her arm. Jasper knew what would happen if they got to the parking lot. They were going to be shot and killed. Some guys that knew Jasper saw the interaction and knew it didn't look right. They walked up to Jasper and engaged in small talk. One of the Mexicans was about to pull his gun out when Renee stuck him in the eye with her car keys. Jasper hit the other guy and a huge fight ensued. Jasper and his friends were able to get the gun away from the Mexicans and beat them up. When they saw security coming everybody ran away.

After the fight at the Plaza, Jasper was nervous and jumpy. Everywhere he went he always looked over his shoulders. Some how Lonnie found out about the fight and reached out to Jasper. He told him that the Mexicans probably wouldn't stop looking for him because they thought he set them up. Lonnie said he felt sorry for Jasper and wanted to help him. Sure he did, they always do. But he wanted Jasper's help again. Lonnie learned that had taken over when Pacman went missing. Jasper worked with Lonnie for a little while but abruptly went into hiding and moved to the suburbs.

Jasper claimed he wanted to be normal again. He wanted to get out of the streets. He had been in the streets long enough and was tired of running and dealing with the police. Jasper wanted to raise his daughter in a safe and loving environment. He didn't feel safe working at Walgreens any more. He felt vulnerable and was suspicious of everyone. If the Mexicans could find him at the Plaza, they would eventually find him at Walgreens. So he quit. He tried working at other jobs but couldn't stay focused. He felt like he was in over his head and wanted a change.

Chapter 22

When Jasper went to the suburbs, he took most of the money he'd made when he sold drugs. Renee had the rest of it. Since he didn't work at Walgreens anymore he thought he'd return to his first love. He applied to be a cook at a fast-food restaurant. He didn't make much money but it gave him something to do and he thought about opening up his own restaurant. The owner took a liking to him and taught him the business. Jasper was a quick learner and the business thrived while he was there.

One afternoon Jasper was cleaning up, taking garbage to the alley when he noticed some guys selling drugs. He stood there for a few minutes and watched how they operated. He saw all the people that were coming to buy whatever it was that they were selling and thought, "Wow! What a waste. These guys don't know what they're doing. Why are they making their customers wait like that? " Most times the customers got tired of waiting and left.

A few days later, when he was at work, he recognized that one of the guys who was on the street selling came into the restaurant. He struck a conversation with a guy name Dino and wanted to offer him some advice. "I'm not trying to get in your business, but I saw you guys dealing the other day.

Y'all got quite a faithful clientele. You had so many people coming and it seemed like they got tired of waiting and left. I see where you could benefit so much better if you tweaked your operation just a little. bit." The guy should have been suspicious but he seemed genuinely interested in learning something new. Jasper continued, "People want to be served and be on their way. They don't want to be standing around. What you should do is put your product in a discarded fast-food bag or potato chip bag and throw it to the ground to make it look like garbage. That way when your customers come all you have to do is go to that bag, get out what they want, and send them on their way. You gotta trust me with this."

The next day Jasper saw the guys out there again but they couldn't seem to grasp the concept. So after he got off work he walked over to the block to talk to Dino. When Dino saw him, he walked over to Jasper and gave him some dap. Jasper watched them for a few transactions and saw all the customers that came and went in a short amount of time. Again, he offered them some advice. "Put ten bags of weed in this potato chip bag and ten more in this other bag." Jasper took the bags half way down the block and put them down. They looked like ordinary pieces of garbage randomly thrown on the ground. If the police did come on the block all the guys had on them was small amounts of cash and it wasn't illegal to have cash. They didn't have to worry about anybody picking up the bags because they were the only ones on the block. And they didn't have to run into a building every time a customer came to buy weed. People weren't standing around waiting. Once they finally embraced that concept, they couldn't help but to keep watching the bags of weed.

Seeing that weed out there, unattended, made them anxious. But Jasper assured them that it wasn't going anywhere. "Stop looking at the bag. If the police see you watching it, they're gonna know something." They appreciated the advice and although Jasper worked about twelve hours a day at the restaurant, he still found time to hang out with them. His declaration that he wanted to go straight and get out of the streets was over. He was back!

Chico was one of the men who hung out and sold weed with the guys. One day he was high and got into a fight with his girlfriend. She asked him the leave, go somewhere and sleep it off but he insisted on picking a fight with her. She called the police just to have him removed from her house but he was so belligerent that they were going to arrest him for disorderly conduct. When they patted him down for a weapon, they found several bags of weed in his pocket. It was only a small amount of weed and they wanted to see if they could work and get some information from him. He told them about Jasper and the changes he made to their operation. On the day they went looking for Jasper he was sitting in one of the guy's cars drinking and smoking. They recovered several dozen bags of weed in disposed bags all up and down the block. Jasper was subsequently named the mastermind and the head of the case. He reached out to Lonnie, who was now working a joint task force with the Chicago Police Department and the DEA. Lonnie was able to get the charges against Jasper dropped. But of course, it came with a price. There was something about Jasper that Lonnie really liked. Lonnie made Jasper an offer he should've ran away from and never agreed to. He wanted Jasper to continue working for him. He offered to let Jasper sell only marijuana in exchange for continued cooperation and Jasper would be free from prosecution. In his new role with the DEA he had the power to make those kinds of deals as long as it was only weed, he did not want to break the law by violating the Hobbs Act. Jasper was officially on the unofficial payroll with the Feds. And he was back on the move again, this time back to Chicago.

CHAPTER 23

Edie was home one evening when out of the blue Jasper called her. He said he wanted, needed, to talk to her. She told him that she was home and invited him to the house. He asked her if Ella was there and she said she wasn't.

When she saw him, she noticed that he was now bigger and taller and had matured since she last saw him. When he walked into the house, he hugged her, kissed her on the cheek, looked around and took a seat. Edie went into her bedroom and came back with some weed for them to smoke. Then she went into the kitchen and brought back some beers. He talked about how the house looked different since he'd last seen it. "Have you heard from your brother?" She said she hadn't. After a few more minutes of small talk, he broke down and bawled like a baby. He told her everything that he had been through in the last couple of years including the truth about the work he did, was doing, for Lonnie. But he insisted that he never told on Pacman. He said that Lonnie had him by the balls but claimed that he was tired of being in the streets and wanted to go legit but didn't know of any other way to make it. They sat and talked for a while, reminiscing about the good times they had. Edie knew Jasper. She knew where he was going with this talk. She knew what he wanted and she was all in. And then he said it, "I wanna come back. I want back in. I learned a lot in the last couple of years. I know I can do it. We can thrive with the shop and we can buy more buildings. You, me, and Ella, all in business again. Edie, please think about it. Plus there is somebody I want you to meet. We became really close and he will be an asset. You're gonna like him. His name is Turtle."

When he ran from Lonnie and to the suburbs, he also ran out on them. He left them to fend for themselves. Edie told him that her and Ella struggled for a few years but they managed. She knew he could help them, not only get caught up and out of debt, but also get ahead. There was something about Jasper. She trusted him because he was like a brother to them but she knew she had to talk to Ella first. Ella still held a grudge against him for what she thought his role was in what happened to their brother and for running out on them. Edie would work on Ella and knew getting her on board would take some convincing. After a couple hours of drinking, smoking, and eating, Ella came home. Jasper left.

Eventually they agreed to partner up with Jasper and almost immediately they saw profits. Edie still managed the shop and they expanded by putting in two barber chairs and a nail salon. The money that Jasper made from selling weed, he put into the shop and they even bought several more two-flats. They were very prudent when it came to spending money. Their clientele picked up.

Edie had a friend who lived down the street from her and she was looking for a good beautician. She was separated from her unfaithful husband who was a cop. Edie invited her to the shop to get her hair done and when Jasper saw how smart, classy, and beautiful she was he tried to impress her by flashing that cash around. She was out of his league and he was way in over his head. They dated briefly while she was separated from her husband until she cut him off. She claimed to not be impressed with the money and said it was only a fling, whatever the hell that meant. He was Thug Life but she wanted the Fresh Prince.

Chapter 25

One evening Edie was doing Carla's hair when Jasper and Turtle came into the shop. When Carla saw Jasper she almost jumped out of the chair. When Edie was finally finished, Carla ran and hugged and kissed him. They sat down in the chairs talking and rubbing each other's thighs. Turtle showed Edie a joint and they went outside in the back to smoke. Edie first went in the office and grabbed a couple of beers.

A few minutes later Edie and Turtle heard a loud commotion in the shop. Turtle opened the door and saw a fight. He ran in with Edie right behind him and saw Jasper fighting somebody. Turtle ran past Carla who was lying motionless on her stomach. Turtle jumped on the guy's back but was tossed off like a doll. Edie went to check on Carla, turned her over and saw that she had a swollen, closed, blackened eye. Edie pulled her to safety and went to the bathroom to get a towel for her eye. Ella came in and yelled for them to stop. Several police officers also came in right behind her. Ella saw that Yunus was beating up Jasper and Turtle and said, "Yunus! Yunus, baby, boo, please calm down. It's gonna be alright." all while rubbing his head. Carla turned to look at them and said, "Bitch, how do you know my husband? And why are you calling him boo?" Turtle said, "That's your husband? That's the dude who's been following me around." When he heard Ella's voice, he calmed down long enough to let the police handcuff him. Yunus leaned into Jasper, who was laying on the ground, and said, "I should have put a bullet in your head that night. I should have finished your ass off when I had the chance."

The shop was a mess. When they took Yunus to the police car, he identified himself and told them he was a Chicago police officer. There were several squad cars doubled-parked in front of the shop all with their lights still flashing. There were also several dozen people looking into the shop.

The sergeant interviewed Yunus and asked him what happened. Yunus said he was driving by the shop and saw his wife's car parked out front. He did a U-turn and pulled in front of the shop. He looked in and saw her hugging and kissing another man. He left his van in the middle of the street, with the engine still running, and ran inside. He said he just snapped when he saw Jasper playing with Carla's titties.

The sergeant went back inside the shop and asked anyone if they wanted to press charges. Nobody did. Jasper, Carla, and Turtle also all refused medical attention. A report was filled out for the extensive damage done to the shop. Yunus was arrested that night but his process was expedited. He asked the sergeant to park his van and give the keys to Ella.

Turtle drove Carla home. Edie, Ella, and Jasper cleaned the shop and had a good talk to air their differences.

On her way home that night, Edie stopped by Savanna's house and told her everything that happened. When she left, Savanna called and told me everything.

Carla found another beautician and no longer messed around with Jasper. She left Yunus and started dating another drug dealer. Ella and Yunus became a couple. Eventually I moved back home.

One day I was in the liquor store, the same one I confronted Jasper at, and saw him and Turtle come in. I was at the counter with my fifth of Crown Royal and they went to the back of the store. They were at refrigerator when they looked up and noticed me. After the cashier rang me up, I blew them a kiss and walked out.

On several occasions I had this crazy dream. I got into an incident with a guy who was high on something and he wouldn't stop walking towards me. I pulled out my gun but he still wouldn't stop. He pulled something to attack me with and when I tried to shoot him my gun wouldn't fire. I had to fight this guy and he was really strong but eventually I won. When I talked to the investigators or the lawyers who represented me, I felt like the guy didn't believe my story and didn't really have my back. He was just going through the motions.

The End...

Made in the USA
Monee, IL
16 July 2022